Austin dreamed of fire that night.

In his dream, a little kid who loved hiding places fell asleep inside bleached bones of driftwood. Gasoline poured down and drenched the child, and Austin could see the face as the child burned, and it was somebody he knew, and Austin woke up sick and shivering, blankets on the floor, window open to a cold April dawn.

It's only a dream, he said to himself. Nobody died in the fire. Nobody even got a blister in the Good Shepherd fire.

He couldn't get warm.

He couldn't go back to sleep.

He lay flat on his back and reviewed the minute, or eternity, they had spent in the triangular prison beneath the chained exit. Crouched between Chamique and Macey, knowing the next smoke-laden breath would kill him, he had had only one syllable in his head.

No.

Caroline Cooney lives in Westbrook, Connecticut, and is the author of many novels for young readers.

BURNING UP

Caroline B. Cooney

MACMILLAN CHILDREN'S BOOKS

First published 1999 by Delacorte Press, a division of Bantam Doubleday
Dell Publishing Group Inc, USA

First published in the UK 2000 by Macmillan Children's Books
a division of Macmillan Publishers Limited
25 Eccleston Place, London SW1W 9NF
Basingstoke and Oxford
www.macmillan.com

Associated companies throughout the world

ISBN 0 330 39104 6

3 5 7 9 8 6 4

A CIP catalogue record for this book is available from
the British Library.

Typeset by SX Composing DTP, Rayleigh, Essex
Printed and bound in Great Britain by Mackays of Chatham plc, Kent

1

Macey dashed out of the high school, filled with the energy of Friday afternoon. She always had to run towards the weekend. The first thing she did on Friday was put distance between herself and the school. Macey was good at school, had friends, liked her teachers – and yet the end of every school week was such a relief.

Around her, sports teams were piling into vans and buses: tennis, baseball, golf and swim teams. Kids with cars shot out of the student parking lot, windows down, so everybody could shout to everybody else.

'Hey, Mace!' came two voices. 'Want a ride?' Macey's best friends, Lindsay and Grace, leaned out the window of a Volvo. Grace's mother had come to pick them up.

'I'm walking, thanks!' yelled Macey.

'Oh, right, it's Friday,' said Lindsay, rolling her eyes. 'She's got her short cuts to take.'

'Oh, brother,' said Grace, laughing out the car window. 'Being a juvenile again?'

Grace's mother blew a kiss to Macey, and they drove on. Macey waved no to the driver of her own school bus. It was a three-mile hike to her grandparents', but Macey took short cuts. Her route was closer to a mile and a half, and if she ran, she could make it in twenty minutes. What the run really did was cut her off from school, making the weekend clean and separate and safe. Macey cut through the golf course, cut through the woods and behind the old supermarket, through back-yards and finally through the swamp.

The swamp wasn't a hundred feet across, and it wasn't a block long, but it had the strength of a canyon. Nobody but Macey ever crossed it.

A few years ago, she'd dragged boards into the swamp to give herself a path over the wettest parts. She hopped on the edge of the first board to be sure it wouldn't split when she put her weight on it.

From a hundred yards away drifted the rich scent of ocean: mudflats and fish and salt water. It was a warm-weather smell. Last week had been March, when school was a thing that would last for ever – but today it was the first week in April, and Macey could shade her eyes and catch a glimpse of summer.

Beyond the swamp was the old stone foundation of a barn. Come summer, wild roses and tiger lilies would make it a sunken garden. Macey was not basically a sitting-down person, but she loved to sit here. It was peaceful. Even in early April, the sun warmed the stones.

Back when there were horses, all these old shorefront houses had had stables. This one, turned into a garage and apartment, had burned when Macey's mother was a girl. Supposedly a man had been in it at the time. When Macey was very little, she'd been afraid of the foundation, because what if the body was still there, waiting for her to find the bones?

But now, at fifteen and a half, she found the idea of discovering bones appealing, like archaeology or journalism.

Ten seconds was plenty of time to sit and consider the olden days. Macey jumped up and cut across the backyards of Shell Beach to her grandparents' house.

Her parents were staying in New York City for dinner. This was good. Mom and Dad were so exhausted at the end of a week that they were useless; on Fridays they just plopped down and faded away, while the television droned and the pizza got cold.

Macey came in Nana and Papa's back door. Her grandparents' back porch was a large glassed-in room, sagging with piles of stuff. There were broken china cups filled with beach glass. There were collections of knotty driftwood and yellow seashells. There were old bathing suits, hung up to dry when Macey was six, or twelve, and never worn again, because Mom bought new ones that weekend. There were magazines that somebody meant to clip something from and lawn chairs somebody meant to repair. There were old golf clubs and new fishing rods and an outboard motor.

Hot cinnamon smells drifted out from the kitchen. Nana and Papa were baking. Food was the centrepiece of their lives. They watched all the TV cooking shows and quoted the great chefs as if they were family friends. They greeted Macey with hugs and kisses and went straight to the crucial topic: what to have for dinner.

'Three-cheese pasta?' suggested Papa. Papa had very high blood pressure and cholesterol, but he didn't care;

3

he ate whatever he felt like. He usually felt like eating a lot.

'No, dear, I found luscious asparagus in the market this morning,' said Nana. 'We'll have asparagus omelettes.' Nana ate more than Papa, and together they made a very roly-poly couple. They were even fatter in their red-and-white-striped French chef aprons.

'Asparagus. Yuck,' said Macey. 'It's tall, thin slime.'

Two sets of blue eyes turned on her. Two identical frowns beneath snowy white hair. 'You walk the dogs,' ordered Nana. 'And we'll decide the menu,' said Papa.

Zipper was an old collie, tired and lame, and the leash was not needed, because he would never stray from her side. Zipper liked to walk down to the sandy edge and sniff the salt water, maybe think about fish for a minute or two, and then totter home.

Moose was a chocolate Lab so large they had respelled his name from (chocolate) Mousse. Macey and Moose would fly down Shell Road, Macey more on the leash than Moose. If Macey didn't take care of Moose's exercise, nobody would, because her grandparents had pretty much surrendered on the exercise front.

Macey took each dog separately, five minutes for Zipper and half an hour for Moose. Back in the kitchen, her grandparents were between cooking shows, and so they turned to their second favourite subject: what Macey was up to.

'We have to do a local history paper,' said Macey. 'When Mrs Johnson assigned it this morning, it felt like a ten-ton truck driving over my shoulders. But I ran all

4

the way here, and now I think it might be OK.'

'Tomorrow morning we'll go to the library and dig for a topic,' said Papa, waving a sifter. Flour dusted his face.

'Papa, I'm not *that* excited about it. Anyway,' she said gloomily, 'tomorrow I have Saturday Group.'

There was an expedition arranged, and they were to meet at 8.30 a.m. Macey did not feel like showing up. Saturday Group was hard. Volunteer work was supposed to make you feel wonderful, but Macey just came home feeling guilty. She was not in a Saturday Group mood. She was in a sleep late, watch cartoons, eat stacks of waffles and do nothing mood.

Nana rolled a lemon around the counter, softening it up before slicing it. 'Did you remember that the first beach bonfire is tonight?'

'No, I didn't. Ooooh, that's wonderful! It's good I'm spending the night.' Macey loved the first bonfire. It meant spring had come, and the window was open to summer: long, slow, hot summer. Sailing and crabbing, picnics and relatives.

Shell Beach was a crescent of sand and granite outcroppings, with twisty pines and tawny marsh grass. Only people who lived on Shell Road could use the beach, but they hardly ever did. People paid a million dollars for beach rights, but they didn't go to the beach. They just liked knowing it was there.

The little beach attracted debris. Tree trunks and broken moorings, Clorox bottles and smashed Styrofoam picnic baskets washed up. Every spring, the residents of Shell Beach would carry away the garbage and prepare the wood for a beach bonfire. Branches and broken oars and planks from hurricane-wrecked docks were piled tepee fashion, eight or ten feet tall. The tepee was built way down on the sand, where it wouldn't matter how high the flames were or whether sparks flew; nothing was around to catch fire.

'Did you buy lots of marshmallows?' asked Macey.

'Of course I bought lots of marshmallows,' said Nana. 'That's been my job for fifty years and I haven't forgotten yet.'

Macey set the table. Dinner here was leisurely, at a beautiful table with fresh flowers. Nana and Papa were never in a rush. Perhaps they had rushed earlier in life, but they were over it now. They used cloth napkins, which they ironed, and silver, which they polished.

This was totally the opposite of home, where her parents ate off paper plates. This was supposed to be a secret from Nana and Papa, who felt they had failed as parents. Their daughter – their own child, Cordelia, this defective stranger – used paper plates at dinner. As for cooking, Macey's parents hardly ever did such a thing. They lived on take-out.

Macey had her own bedroom at her grandparents' house and kept plenty of clothes there. She knew kids who had two homes and hated it, because it was from divorce, but she had two homes and it was perfect.

Her parents loved their jobs, and wanted to be the best and the first. They lived here because it was an easy commute into New York City by train, and Macey could grow up in a house with a yard and a dog, and her grandparents would be right down the road to pitch in.

Her mother was in marine insurance, oil tankers and stuff, and her father in banking, mostly foreign loans.

They were wildly proud of Macey, but they were wildly proud of themselves, too, so it was relaxing to be around Nana and Papa, who just muttered and rolled out pastry. She was the only grandchild, and they adored her. In their eyes, she was the most intelligent, interesting, beautiful and talented girl in America. When Macey reached high school, and there was a lot of competition for those slots, she found out Nana and Papa were wrong: she was not the most intelligent, interesting, beautiful and talented girl in her class, let alone America. But still, it was nice to hear.

'For my local history paper, I was thinking of doing the construction collapse,' said Macey. 'Remember how eight floors fell in? Think of the photographs and sound effects!' She was sure the newspaper had done a special issue, which would certainly make the research quicker.

'That was seven years ago,' said Nana. 'The history of this town begins in 1652.'

'And we're all very proud of the settlers of 1652,' agreed Macey, 'but things happened in the nineteen nineties too.'

'They aren't history!'

'They will be eventually,' said Macey. 'You just have to wait awhile.'

Nana slid the perfect nine-egg omelette neatly on to a serving platter and divided it in three. Macey decided she could eat around the asparagus. They sat down at the table and asked the Lord's blessing.

Macey broke off a piece of brioche, a soft, buttery bread that was Papa's this-month favourite to bake.

'How do you do a term paper with sound effects?' said her grandfather.

'If you get an A, you can put your paper on the school web page,' said Macey.

This was the first time Macey had ever seen boys thrilled by a history assignment. Normally, a boy sadly wrote his name all crammed up into the corner of a blank piece of paper and then watched his signature, hoping the letters would spread and fill the rest of the page. This condition could last for days, until the boy finally admitted that letter spread was not a known scientific possibility. Gloomily, and acting betrayed, the boy would finally start to write.

But this was different. Their papers would go on-line.

'In *school* you have a *web page*?' said Nana. She flounced in her chair, a technique Macey wanted to learn: how to look huffy while sitting down.

'It's not evil,' said Macey, laughing. 'We're not making rugs out of endangered animals or exchanging recipes for dolphin sandwiches.'

'You like computers,' accused Nana.

'I love computers. I love the Internet. Except now that I consider it, I'll skip sound effects. They take too long and people would give up.'

'Your parents allow you to use the Internet?' said Papa, scandalized.

'Now, Papa. Who else's parents would be involved?' Macey didn't usually give her grandparents an opening to discuss Mom and Dad's lifestyle. Mom and Dad avoided confrontation by not visiting a whole lot. They were only two miles away, and they saw Nana and Papa barely once a month.

'Or maybe the fire,' said Macey. 'That would be a good story.'

'What fire, dear?' said Nana.

'The one that burned the Demitroffs' barn down. I was just resting on the foundation this afternoon. That old arson. With the man trapped inside. I could read old newspapers and go to the fire department and get old records.'

There was an odd pause. It was long enough for Macey to look up from her excavation of asparagus out of her omelette and see that her grandmother and grandfather were looking at each other and not at her.

'Macey, that isn't history,' said her grandfather. 'That isn't anything. It's just an old building that isn't there any more.'

'And nobody was trapped inside,' said Nana. 'Is Austin going tomorrow to the Saturday Group? I am so interested that he is still living here. He's such a cutie. Do you know any details yet?'

Austin's grandparents, the Fents, lived across Shell Road from Macey's grandparents. Macey and Austin hardly knew each other, although he had visited Shell Beach for a month every summer. Austin was Macey's age but always acted either ten years older or ten years younger, so no matter how cute he was, Macey had not bothered to get to know him better. She didn't know what he was doing here for the school year. Couldn't be anything good. You didn't skip your sophomore year at your own high school in Chicago with your lifelong friends and then go live with your grandparents in another state just for the fun of it.

Nana was as fond of gossip as she was of food. 'Even when I ask the gentlest, most neighbourly questions,' she said, hurt to be left out of such an important loop, 'his grandparents change the subject. I assume his mother is behaving badly and they are ashamed of her. I cannot believe you have gone to school with this boy for so many months and not found out why he's living here.'

Austin was not in any classes with Macey, although he had several of the same teachers. He'd been here since November, and now it was April, and she had no clue. 'He's probably going to Saturday Group,' she said. 'He went last month when they did the soup kitchen.'

Macey had not done the soup kitchen. She hated things where people were sad and grimy and lost.

But tomorrow's field trip was painting the Sunday school rooms at their sister church, Good Shepherd, an inner-city church to which they gave a little money and their old furniture. Macey detested art class, but she loved painting big things, like walls. An art teacher had sketched a master plan for the project. The rooms would be daffodil yellow and sunset orange, barn red and ocean blue. Crayon colours, to brighten the dark.

'Then that's your assignment,' said Nana, meaning Austin. 'Research the situation. Report back.'

In their attempt to divorce, Austin's mother and father

10

had become bickering, screaming children. It was unbearable. His perfectly nice, intelligent, good parents yelling foul names, setting traps for each other, ambushing each other with legal problems. With all that fighting, they had no time to raise a son. When Grandmother and Grandfather suggested that Austin stay with them until things cooled down, he was glad to put distance between himself and his shrieking parents.

The shock was, his mother and father were also glad. Glad to wave goodbye so they could concentrate on their war.

The second shock was how fast the first shock wore off.

He arrived too late in the school year to be in any fall sport or get a part in the drama production. Austin had never been able to sit still, so he needed a job, any job, and he agreed to get advertising for the play programme. Kids crept up to him in school and whispered that they were responsible for selling two ads, but they couldn't do it, they couldn't go up to strangers and beg; would Austin do it for them?

He set a school record, more sales than anybody had accomplished in the 110-year history of the high school. His math teacher adjusted it for inflation and Austin was still the highest.

So he was successful, a hero, and had more poise than anybody in the entire high school. Not bad.

The best thing, though, was Grandfather.

Grandfather had owned a small bank, which was kind of a neat thought, your own personal bank, but it had been bought out and merged into an enormous

Boston bank. Grandfather was still involved, and at seventy-nine had not retired.

Austin felt as if Grandfather had been waiting for years, needing a grandson to do things with. They went to air shows together, they went to ice hockey games, they were restoring an old wooden boat. When Austin mentioned his lifelong dream of hiking the Appalachian Trail, Grandfather said he'd always wanted to do that, and so they were planning to do some of the New England section this summer, a day or two at a time.

Grandfather wanted to rebuild the old stone wall that divided his property from the Demitroffs'. Shifting a couple hundred feet of fieldstone was no minor event. So they'd joined a gym and were working out.

Austin's mind was a snow flurry of plans. He had a hard time falling asleep at night because his thoughts about the next day wouldn't lie down and relax. When his parents called (which wasn't often), he was startled. Oh, yeah, he would think. Parents.

And now, with spring here, plans had to be made for the summer.

He could not imagine telling his father – Dad, I'm busy. Can't fit you in.

Or his mother – Mom, I like your parents. I'm staying here.

This was a problem he needed to move to the front of his planning, but he kept forgetting. After school, which would have been good thinking time, he rarely took the bus, but ran. It was three miles from the high school to his grandparents'. He loved to time himself.

The Fents finished dinner. Their meals were solid

and predictable. The rib roast; the leftovers from the rib roast. The roast chicken; the leftovers from the chicken. That was four nights right there, and they'd go out the other three. Austin's grandmother instructed him about the coat he must wear to keep off the evening chill, and said to her husband, 'We've been having these bonfires how many years now, dear?'

'Half a century, I suppose,' said Grandfather.

Half a century! It seemed an impossible length of time, a stretch from here to a comet's tail. Austin was fascinated by the comet of 1997. It shivered him that a comet nobody expected and nobody had predicted, captured by the minds and eyes of a man named Hale and a man named Bopp, had suddenly stained the night sky. On clear nights, he liked to walk out on the farthest tip of beach and examine the sky.

'Exactly what are the plans for Saturday Group?' asked his grandmother.

'We're painting Sunday school rooms at Good Shepherd,' he told his grandparents. 'We get eight hours' credit. Two adults, ten kids.' One would be Macey Clare. Austin could not understand how he was living across the street from Macey's second home and he never saw her and could not seem to get to know her. The church van held fifteen, and his theory was that he would manage to sit with her. (It wouldn't happen. Macey would be escorted by her girlfriends Lindsay and Grace.)

The high school had a community service rule: you had to do fifteen hours each year. Graff, the school media specialist, had organized Saturday Group

13

through the church, but you could get community service credit whether you had anything to do with the church or not. Saturday Group did one-shot stuff: serving at a soup kitchen in Bridgeport, taking inner-city kids from Hartford on a river expedition, working on park restoration in New Haven. Austin had done everything. He liked how you put in your eight hours and you drove home feeling good and slept at night knowing you had done your share. He was way over his hours requirement. Several guys at school had approached him on the subject of buying his volunteer time, but nobody had figured out how to accomplish this.

'Good Shepherd?' repeated his grandfather. 'No, Austin, I think not. Fifty years ago it was a beautiful building in a beautiful city, but there has been too much demographic change. Terrible neighbourhood. Drug- and crime-ridden. I do not want you there.'

'Grandfather, nothing's going to happen.'

'Correct, because you are not going.'

Austin knew by now that arguing did not work with Henry Fent. But he could often tease his way out.

So he said, 'What about all that weightlifting you and I have been doing?'

'Some use that will be against drug dealers' guns.'

'I won't be standing on the corner buying crack, Grandfather. I'll be in the church basement slapping paint on the walls.'

'These people should maintain their buildings,' said Grandmother. 'That's the kind of population there now. People who let things go.'

'But I'm the Paint Wizard,' said Austin. 'Two coats from my paintbrush, and those walls will stand for ever.'

The neighbours gathered on the sand. It was cloudy. No moon, no stars, no comet. The wind was high and waves sloshed without rhythm, smashing against hidden rocks in the shallow cove.

Austin was wearing a heavy canvas jacket with fleece lining. It had great pockets. He usually kept a Swiss Army knife in one; wallet zipped inside another; pen, Post-its, all that school stuff in a third. He liked the weight and the safety of his possessions in pockets. Tonight he had only the knife.

The wood for the bonfire seemed to form a tiny shelter for some little kid to hide in. When he was little, Austin had liked hiding. There was no trunk, closet or cabinet bottom where he could not curl up. Once he'd stuffed himself into his dad's golf bag.

It made him feel good to have a happy kid memory. Actually, most of his kid memories were happy, and it chewed him up that his parents did not put more value on the happy memories the three of them shared.

Mr Macey (Macey's grandfather; Austin liked how her first name was her grandparents' last name) appeared with a can of gasoline. It was one of those red metal cans you filled at the gas station. Dented, scratched, discoloured. It held two gallons. From the way he swung it, it wasn't very full. The beach was dark, so Austin's grandfather turned up his heavy flashlight to light Mr Macey's way.

Putnam Macey and Henry Fent had been friends for seventy-five years. Austin could not get hold of that: seventy-five years.

And the contrast between his grandparents and Macey's! Austin's grandmother, Monica Fent, still weighed what she had in high school and took Jazzercise classes three times a week. Henry Fent was seventy-nine and could nearly hold his own with Austin. Macey's grandparents, however, took naps for afternoon exercise and never seemed to think beyond the next meal. It mystified Austin that Mr and Mrs Macey could feel they had interesting lives when all they were really doing was rolling out pastry dough.

Mrs. Macey sat way up on the dry sand on a stone as big as a wheelbarrow. Austin knew the stone: it had a cupped top that held rainwater like blood for a sacrifice.

He spotted Macey. In the path of several flashlights, she looked strange and shadowed. He could see only half of her, as if she had been cut vertically, like a paper doll. She too wore a canvas jacket unzipped, and it flailed in the wind, and her hair went spinning over her eyes. He drifted over to her, because they were the only people under forty.

She smiled. 'Hey, Aus.'

'Hey, Mace.'

They had never had more conversation than this.

He waved at the woodpile. 'I didn't know what all that wood was stacked up for,' he said, although of course he'd been at plenty of summer bonfires. It was just something to say to a girl. 'I figured it was some sort of sand temple.'

'Oh, absolutely. Driftwood worship is a real problem around here,' said Macey. 'People guard their children against it.'

They laughed.

Austin's grandmother said, 'Good evening, Macey. How are your parents?'

'Fine, thank you,' said Macey.

'Tell your mother we miss her.'

There was a barb in this that Austin could not pick up, but Macey apparently did. She smiled tightly.

'Your parents are so busy, Macey,' said Austin's grandmother.

Austin got it this time. The old Supermom, Superdad problem. Lack of time for children, et cetera. Macey did not look particularly deprived to Austin.

'Mrs Fent,' said Macey, 'do you remember the fire? The one that burned down the barn that belongs to the Demitroffs now?'

The Demitroffs lived next door to his grandparents, but Austin could think of no barn, and definitely no fire. However, Austin had been part of this world only in July, and only as a child, so he knew nothing. The town, its gossip and its people were blanks to him. He waited to hear about the fire.

'Vaguely,' said Austin's grandmother.

Austin was surprised. Nothing in Grandmother's life was vague. She had been an accountant long before women were accountants, chief financial officer for a precision machine company back when the only thing most women were machining was an apron at the sewing machine.

'What year was that fire?' asked Macey.

'Oh, I don't know,' said Monica Fent. 'Ages ago.'

Austin's grandmother was the type who remembered not only the year, but also the day of the week, and if she had just been to the dentist.

Down on the sand, four men circled the pile of wood. They were shadow against shadow. Their silhouettes looked like Druids, ancient priests setting a sacred fire for a sacrifice. In the shroud of dark, Austin could not tell who they were.

One of them lifted the can of gas, flipped the tiny lid on the spout, and poured gasoline up and around and inside the piled timber. Using a pole with a gas-soaked rag tied on, they held a match to the rag. The javelin of fire was speared into the wood, and the fire went up with a roar like powerboats in a race, and the men backed up fast, their hands out, both warming themselves and holding off the enemy. Fire lit sky and water and sand, and the four stood together, their backs to the shore, and they were like statues, dark and unknown but shiny as metal where the fire bronzed them.

'I'm surprised nobody sees this from across the water and calls the fire department,' said Austin.

'They do,' said Macey. 'We have to notify the fire department that we're having a bonfire, or somebody panics and calls 911, and we get fire trucks.'

'It's probably more fun with fire trucks,' said Austin.

'But the firemen get all agitated and they're not your friends any more,' she said.

He laughed. He'd taken Macey's short cuts today,

without letting her see, and had been amazed to find that she was doing some serious trespassing. Not only were there signs – DO NOT ENTER, PRIVATE PROPERTY – twice, Macey had to get over a chain-link fence, and in another place squeeze between strands of barbed wire. It was a whole new view of her.

Mrs Demitroff wandered over to Austin and Macey.

The Demitroffs were in their forties. They had postponed having children; Mrs Demitroff ended up taking fertility pills and now had triplets, age three. Once Mrs Demitroff had actually asked Austin to babysit. He explained to her that he was unreliable and cruel and children had nightmares when they were around him. Mrs Demitroff said she didn't care, she would pay him anything. Austin said he was never going to be for sale where triplets were concerned.

Mrs Demitroff said, 'I looked up the word *bonfire* once. Do you know what it means? Bone fire. It used to be for the burning of corpses.'

'Oh, sweet Mrs Demitroff,' said Macey. 'Is this the kind of bedtime story you tell the triplets?'

'I had hoped to hire you or Austin for my triplets, but no. You are opposed to the care of little children.'

'We're not actually opposed to the care of little children,' said Austin. 'If you want them to have care, go ahead. We just oppose having a share in it.'

'Think of the money I would pay you,' coaxed Mrs Demitroff.

Macey said, 'What do you know about the fire when your stable burned down?'

'Not a thing.' Mrs Demitroff fixed herself a twig for

19

marshmallow toasting. 'It was decades ago. Ancient history.'

Austin whittled down a couple of sticks so there were no twigs poking out the sides and the tops were sharp and pale and clean. He handed one to Macey.

'Aus,' she said, 'you're a prince.'

But there was no meaning in how she said it; she just practised courtesy around her grandparents. Austin knew the habit.

Her hair swirled in the wind and he hoped she would put a rubber band around it before she got near the fire, but she paid no attention to her hair. He imagined making a safe ponytail for her with his fist.

'Here's a better stick, Mrs Demitroff,' said Austin. He was enjoying himself. He liked neighbours. In the city, no matter how harsh the winter – and Chicago winters made Connecticut winters look pretty wimpy – you were always in the midst of your neighbours, but here in the suburbs, neighbours vanished until spring. Now he could imagine spring and summer, full of company, ages three to seventy-nine.

Macey was definitely interested in that old fire. Now she asked Miss Miklowsky, a woman whose wrinkles entered her in a contest for oldest American.

Miss Miklowsky had put three marshmallows on her stick at once. She liked hers burned black, so there was little technique involved – shove it in the flames and let it catch fire, blow it out when cinders start dropping. 'Oh, it was just a stable, Macey. You know, horses. I guess somebody got them out. I don't remember anything about a renter. But I moved here eighteen years

20

ago and you're going back thirty-eight years.'

Macey said, 'Thirty-eight years? Then you know when the fire was?'

'It was 1959.'

'How can you remember that if you weren't even here?' asked Austin.

'There was still talk when I moved to the neighbourhood.'

Must have been some fire if there was still talk nearly twenty years afterwards, thought Austin.

'Talk about what?' said Macey.

Miss Miklowsky tried to remember. But nothing came to her.

Thirty-eight years ago. Austin was sixteen this year. Thirty-eight was more than twice as long as he had been alive. He could readily imagine that a person would remember nothing from thirty-eight years ago. On the other hand, his grandmother could still quote poetry she'd memorized in grammar school, *seventy* years ago.

Austin and Macey circled the fire to find a good toasting spot. Macey's grandmother had patiently toasted her marshmallow to golden perfection. 'Nana, does 1959 sound right?' asked Macey.

'For what, dear?'

'For the fire at the Demitroffs' stable.'

'I'm foggy, dear. These bonfires blend in, you know. Every flame the same as the next.'

Austin's marshmallow was perfect. He showed it to Macey, who thought he was offering it to her, and she ate half his marshmallow off the stick. He ate the other half, and the gooey sweet taste was the taste of summer. 'Why are you interested in the fire, Mace?' asked Austin.

'I need a local history project. Don't you? You have Mrs Johnson, right?'

He nodded. 'I'm going to have a hard time. I'm not local, and I can't work up any excitement about local history.'

'The fire prickled at me,' said Macey. 'I feel itchy from it.'

A horn honked three times, in a rhythmic pattern: short, short, long.

'Oops, it's Mom and Dad,' said Macey. 'Guess I'm not spending the night after all. Bye, Nana, Bye, Papa. Got to run.' She was showered with the goodbyes of neighbours, like falling stars.

'You would think they could bother to get out of the car,' said Macey's grandparents, more loudly than they needed to, 'and come say good evening to us all.'

'Bye, Mace,' said Austin softly. 'See you tomorrow.'

In the flickering light, her smile was just a curve. 'I was going to skip Saturday Group, Aus, but if you go, I'll go.'

She was still holding the marshmallow stick he had whittled for her.

2

'Lindsay, use your head,' said Graff. 'You can't take that designer leather jacket and your mobile phone. You're just setting yourself up.'

'My mother said I have to take the mobile phone, in case we have to call for help.'

'I'll be there,' said Graff. 'You won't need to call for help. We're going to be in a church basement.'

'But the church is in the worst neighbourhood in the whole city,' said Lindsay.

Actually, the kids were pleased to be visiting the worst neighbourhood in the whole city. They lived in a town that had only best neighbourhoods, so danger and poverty intrigued them.

'Isn't anybody else coming?' said Graff frowning at Austin, Macey, Lindsay and Grace. 'We had six more signed up and a parent.'

'It's too pretty out,' said Grace. 'The others are skipping.'

It was a beautiful day. The sun was shimmering on the first unfurling leaves, and the green fringe of new spring smelled fresh and exciting.

The church van held fifteen, and the four kids crowded together to talk while Graff drove. Behind them were gallons of paint and a cardboard box of brushes, masking tape, rollers, pans, rags and extra old T-shirts. A donor had sent along three beanbag chairs that were still serviceable and not leaking any of their little white pellets. Macey was glad they were bringing gifts. She liked thinking of children curled up in those soft old beanbags.

Under her feet was an enormous restaurant-size can that had once held some amazing amount of peaches. A kindergarten teacher had been saving old crayons and sent them along for the children at Good Shepherd.

Macey's heart sank. These crayons were short, stubby ruins. Nobody ever wanted a broken old crayon with the paper wrapping gone. Everybody always wanted new crayons. Everybody always wanted a whole box of new crayons.

When they finally reached the right turnpike exit, Lindsay said, 'We're getting off *here*? This is where my mother always says, "We better not break down now, or we'll be dead."'

They laughed.

The neighbourhood off the exit ramp was just buildings, most of them not occupied. It was a business thoroughfare without businesses. This was a city without a single department store. Nobody would shop here, because they couldn't park. It was too dangerous.

Macey looked down each intersection at old brick row houses, which must have been romantic once; as if Mary Poppins had wheeled a pram on that pavement and scolded a little girl in shiny patent leather shoes under a cherry tree. Now, sections of brick had fallen away, windows had been broken, plywood had been nailed over some of the doors. Dogs barked behind high grilles that enclosed tiny bare dirt yards.

Macey shuddered. Imagine growing up here.

Several blocks after that was a park. Or what had been a park. The wooden seats had been torn away from the metal frames of the benches, so there was nothing to sit on. A bronze statue of a horse and rider was covered with graffiti. The flower beds were littered with old clothes. A minute later it clicked through to Macey that the old clothes were occupied by sleeping people.

The church parking lot was surrounded by high chain-link, and rolls of razor wire glittered on top of that. The minister was waiting for them, and when the van had driven in, he closed the gates and padlocked them.

'Good morning,' he said. 'I am Reverend Warren.' He was tall and heavy and dark-skinned, and his voice came out slowly, as if he really enjoyed meeting Saturday Group and wanted his syllables to last. 'I welcome you in the name and spirit of Jesus Christ.'

Nobody would have said such a thing in Macey's church. But it worked for him. He smiled, and they shook hands and introduced themselves and headed inside just as a man on the pavement began peeing on the church wall.

Inside, the Church of the Good Shepherd was old and decrepit, but it was familiar. The layout, the style, the use of each room were things Macey knew well. She felt comfortable in the building.

She did not feel as comfortable with her painting

partners, a group of teenagers from Good Shepherd: Venita, Isaiah, Chamique and Davonn. Macey had known very few black kids.

'Macey?' said Venita. Her hair was in dozens of braids hardly wider than a pencil lead, the braids gathered in exotic loops and whorls. She wore old clothes for painting and looked fragile inside a droopy faded shirt. 'Hi. You and me, we're doing the yellow room. Come on.'

Isaiah beckoned to Austin. Macey thought the two of them would be a good match if they wrestled; they were built the same – stocky, broad-shouldered, not perfectly proportioned.

Lindsay and Grace did not want to be separated, so Davonn said he would paint alone and the two girls could both paint with Chamique. Chamique said nothing. She looked at Venita, who shrugged. Venita turned to Macey. 'Macey's a store, isn't it? Used to be one here.'

'They spell it differently,' said Macey. 'But it is a store.' She could think of nothing else to say. She could tell that Davonn was hurt and Chamique was angry, and she did not know what to do about it. Lindsay and Grace weren't easy to lecture. And it wasn't Macey's fault that the other six Saturday Group kids hadn't come and Davonn had no painting partner. Luckily, Austin began talking about baseball, and it turned out that he and Davonn and Isaiah were equally concerned about the Red Sox's chances this year.

They passed offices and a parlour and went down a set of stairs. 'Mmm, cinnamon,' said Macey. 'What's cooking?'

'Snacks for us painters,' said Venita. 'My grandmother's cinnamon-icing sticky buns. Been using her recipe thirty years here. It's not a church supper without Dorothy Edna's cinnamon-icing sticky buns.'

'They smell done to me,' said Aus. He grinned and planted himself in front of the open kitchen doors.

'You gotta earn 'em,' said Isaiah, pushing him forward.

They passed through a half-court gymnasium that was mainly beneath the ground, and this was the room where Graff would be working; scaffolding was prepared and tarpaulins covered the floor. Several grown-ups paused in their preparations to shake hands with Graff.

Up a half flight of stairs and into a basement hallway were eight little rooms for Sunday school.

'Actually it's for after-school care,' explained Venita. 'The church opens its doors to elementary-school kids from three o'clock till their mamas come for them.' She pointed to the bathroom. 'That's the most important room. Half the school toilets don't have seats and the doors are torn off and they're always out of toilet paper or soap or something, so the kids just hang till they get here.'

'The toilets don't have seats?' said Macey, shuddering. 'Why don't the janitors just replace them?'

'The school got no money for that,' said Venita.

The hallway was damp with its first coat of white primer. The basement smelled so heavily of paint that Macey could hardly breathe.

'See you, Mace,' said Austin, his hand passing over her shoulder. He went on down the hall with Isaiah.

27

Venita waved Macey into the third of the eight little rooms. Dark, sick hospital green covered the walls. 'Our room is two colours of yellow,' said Venita with pleasure. 'Deep yellow up to here, and pale yellow above it. They said it might take four coats to cover. So if it doesn't look right, just keep painting. Isaiah, his room is bright red up to about your waist, and then really wide stripes of purple and indigo. Don't you love that word *indigo*? Doesn't it sound bluer than blue? Wait till you see their paint. I'm not jealous, though, I like our paint best. Our kids are the six-year-olds, and I think they're right for yellow gold. Their kids are ten- to twelve-year-olds, so they can use bigger colours. Don't you think?'

'Yes,' said Macey. She could hardly wait to start transforming the room. She loved to think of six-year-olds here amid the gold.

Venita carefully poured an inch of paint out of a large can and into a flat slanted pan. 'Easier to dip into,' she explained. 'First we paint the whole room the pale yellow, OK?'

'OK.' Macey started. Her brush was a wide foam square with a handle, and the paint slid off and gleamed wetly. Macey did one wall, floor to ceiling, while Venita worked more slowly on moulding and trim. 'Do you live near here?' Macey asked.

'Three blocks. My grandma teaches Sunday school here. I got three little brothers come after school. I work here every afternoon.'

'I've never had a job,' Macey confessed. 'What do you get paid?'

'Paid! Girl, we're not talking money. This is church.'

They painted. The slopping sound of the brushes and the slickery sound of paint as it went on were satisfying. Macey loved how the paint stuck. What an amazing thing paint was – liquid that didn't run, but stuck to your walls and made them beautiful.

Venita said, 'You got a crush on that boy? That one named for Texas?'

Macey laughed. 'Austin. Well, I've thought about it.'

'You can't think about a crush. You have one, or you don't have one.'

'I don't have one, then.'

'You should. He's a cutie.'

'That's what my grandmother says.'

'You live with your grandmother? Me too. My mama's getting well, but she can't help us till she's all well. She did drugs, and they messed her up. She loves us, see, but she can't quite be a mama. So we live with our grandma. How come you live with your grandma?'

Austin and Isaiah walked in before Macey had to come up with an answer. 'Just wanted to check out your colour,' said Austin, looking at their yellow walls.

'Yours isn't as good as ours.'

'I beg your pardon,' said Macey. 'Our colour is sunshine and crowns of gold.'

'Whoa,' said Venita. 'Sounds like Shakespeare.'

'You studying Shakespeare?'

'Yup. Mr Santangelo, he can photocopy a Shakespeare play, see. There aren't enough classroom copies of anything that we can all read the same book, so even though it's American Lit. this year, we're doing *Hamlet*.

The boys love *Hamlet* 'cause everybody dies in the end and the stage is all stabbing and poison.'

'"Oh, I die, Horatio, the potent poison quite o'er-crows my spirit. I cannot live to hear the news from England,"' said Isaiah unexpectedly.

Venita shoved him to the floor, put her foot on his chest and said in a voice as elegant as her hair, '"Now cracks a noble heart. Good night, sweet Prince, and flights of angels sing thee to thy rest."'

'The girls love clutching their hands together and crying, "Good night, sweet Prince,"' explained Isaiah from the floor. 'They don't even let you say your whole speech before they bury you.'

Austin was laughing. He reached a hand down to haul Isaiah up, but Venita seemed reluctant to remove her pink-sneakered foot. 'What does photocopying have to do with it?' asked Austin.

'Copy places won't let you copy a book that's new, so we can only read old, old stuff that they do let you copy,' said Isaiah.

'Here's the part I like in *Hamlet*,' said Venita. 'Where Hamlet says' – and she lowered her voice, drew out her syllables and hissed evilly across the room – '"Tis now the very witching time of night when churchyards yawn and Hell itself breathes out Contagion to this world. Now could I drink hot blood and do such bitter business as the day would quake to look on."' Venita took her pink sneaker off Isaiah's chest. 'See,' she said in an everyday voice, 'that's right outside the door. Bitter business the day would quake to look on.'

The words crept backwards through Macey's heart,

breathing contagion. *When churchyards yawn*. What a horrible image – churches paying no attention while the day quaked.

'Don't pay her no mind,' said Isaiah, getting up. 'Mr Santangelo, he calls her a romantic.'

Davonn poked his head in. 'You paintin' or what? This ain't Shakespeare.'

For the ceiling, there were fleecy rollers on sticks. Venita and Macey had not the slightest idea how to paint the ceiling and they were both horrified by the possibility of getting paint in their hair. They poked ineffectively as far away from themselves as possible. All they did was smear the ceiling.

'This,' said Macey, 'is pathetic. We have to put something over our hair and do this right. Shower caps would be perfect, but I didn't know enough to bring any.' She choked suddenly on the paint smell and began wheezing and coughing.

Venita rescued Macey's paint pole so nothing would spatter in their hair during a coughing spasm. Then she went down the hall, opened a side door and propped it by wedging rags beneath it. Fresh air whipped around the corner, cool and essential.

When she came back, Macey said, 'I'm like a six-year-old myself. I keep thinking about snack time. Isn't it almost here?'

Venita grinned. 'It's church torture, making you wait for Dorothy Edna's cinnamon-icing sticky buns.'

The fresh air sailed over a pile of empty paint cans. Past a garbage can packed with paint-soaked rags.

31

Around stacks of newspaper. Around a slender oval container of turpentine . . . as flammable a liquid as ever gladdened the heart of an arsonist.

Venita raised her head oddly.

Macey looked at Venita and found herself imitating the movement of Venita's chin, and so the faint smell of smoke entered Macey's nostrils too, and penetrated her brain, and she and Venita stared at each other.

Each girl set her brush down gently, to prevent dripping.

Each girl straightened and went to the door as if caution would prevent the smoke from being real.

They stepped into the narrow hall.

Its first coat of white was still tacky, gleaming like windows in the sun.

To their left were the painters in the last five rooms. Their chatter and the squishy *ploof* of their paint rollers, the slappy back-and-forth of their brushes could be heard. A radio in one room was on a rock station; the radio in another room was tuned to a gospel station; and distantly, a third radio was playing an ad for car radios, which were a good deal at Car Max.

To their right was a grey puff.

It was no more than a cigarette being exhaled.

Venita glared at it and put her hands on her hips.

She was the image of a schoolteacher, gonna march down there and tell off that jerk smoking around paint cans! Where was his brain?

The grey puff turned the corner like a locomotive, and then it was an engine on fire, and the flames took the paint off the wall, and the wind from the outside door flung fire and smoke towards the girls, and Venita screamed, *'Fire!'* and Macey screamed, *'Get Out! Everybody out!'* and they turned left because the fire had captured the right, and by the time Macey and Venita had gone the ten steps to the next Sunday school room, the fire had caught their heels and Macey saw Austin and Isaiah, and then the smoke was upon her and bit her eyes so cruelly she had to close them, and she felt the fire on her back.

Macey looked like some terrible angel in a crown of fire.

In the horror of the moment, Austin could not explain it.

His shout did not reach her, for she was blind and deaf under her own flames.

It was her hair blazing.

She had beautiful hair, a dark rich chestnut, straight and long. She was always putting her hair up in scrunchies or twisting it into a knot she could hold with a pencil stab, then taking it down to make a ponytail in her fingers.

Austin pulled his T-shirt off and, just before the smoke swirled in, yanked it over her head, suffocating the fire and Macey. She fought him, and he yelled at her, rubbing and scraping at her head, pinning her to the wall with his knee so he could put out the fire in her hair.

Lindsay and Grace were screaming uselessly. Davonn and Isaiah were yelling even louder, 'Shut up, shut up!'

Davonn lunged against the panic bar at the exit, and the door opened outward.

'Where's Chamique?' screamed Venita, and Austin shoved Macey through the exit door. Chamique was right behind him; he grabbed the cloth of her shirt and pulled her along.

The smell was horrific.

Burning paint and turpentine did not produce the fine, appetizing smell of barbecues or beach bonfires. It was the smell of fear and death.

The exit did not exit. It opened to a stair and the stair was enclosed by a bulkhead, leaving a tiny triangle of space for them to crouch in. Chamique yanked the door shut after them, to keep the fire and the smoke on the other side.

The door above them did not lift, no matter how hard Austin and Isaiah and Davonn slammed their shoulders into it.

It was completely dark in the triangular space of stair and lid, but not yet very smoky. 'We've got to calm down,' said Austin, who was not calm; who was sick imagining Macey's face from those flames. 'There'll be some sort of lock bar holding the bulkhead doors together. We've got to find it with our fingers.'

'I found it already,' said Isaiah. 'It isn't hooked. But the door still doesn't open. It's padlocked on the outside.'

Nobody said anything to that.

There was nothing to say.

They would die like people in a jar. They would die of smoke, not fire. At least it would be quick, not slow.

'My fault,' said Venita. 'I opened the door.'

'We needed the air,' said Austin.

''Cept there's been an arsonist going after churches,' said Davonn. 'Guy probably looked in, saw turpentine – whatever. One flick of a lighter and we're dead meat.'

Macey's head was actually smoking. She was breathing in her death. *Arson.* Incredibly, her mind moved all the way back to 1959, to the moment when another building and another person had burned.

It wasn't anything, her grandfather had said. Just an old building that isn't there any more.

In a little while I won't be anything, thought Macey. Just a person who isn't here any more.

Distantly she heard Venita say, 'Everybody get down. Air's better close to the bottom. Remember fire drills?'

Macey could not remember fire drills.

She heard Davonn say, 'I hear sirens. We gotta yell, we gotta make them hear us, we gotta be louder.'

The stench of burning paint seemed part of her, as if she were being fired like pottery in a kiln.

3

The sirens got so loud so quickly! Austin thought they must have come from just around the corner. In moments, his pounding upward on the metal doors was equalled by pounding down.

'Door getting hot,' said Chamique. She'd been the last one in and her back was pressed against the door into the church. Austin skimmed his hands behind her and tightened her in against himself, giving her a few inches of space. He could not feel more heat, but he could taste the difference in the air. He held his breath against the smoke.

Up above was scraping and the lunging of metal against metal, and a shower of swear words, and he prayed that whatever was holding the door down could be severed. He thought of the possible tools, and even though he could hear the firemen above them yelling, 'Don't shove up!' he couldn't help it, and neither could Isaiah and Davonn, and they kept shoving up, and suddenly the chain or lock snapped, and the double doors got thrust up so fast Austin was afraid the firemen's chins would be split. But the men leaped back and helped with the doors, and eight teenagers spurted out like water from a hose.

They stood stunned on a pavement. Smoke poured

out after them, and the firemen poured down the stairs after it.

'I'm alive,' Macey whispered. She held out her hands and found that she had no burns, that nothing had happened to her. Venita was staring down at her own hands, and the girls touched fingertips, amazed to be safe.

'We're all alive,' said Austin, counting.

'Leggo my shirt, Texas,' said Chamique.

Austin managed to loosen his grip on her. 'I ain't mad,' she said, grinning at him. 'You can be my fire partner anytime, Texas.'

'Nobody got hurt,' said Isaiah, touching faces and bare arms, reassuring himself that he was right, that no one was hurt.

Lindsay and Grace were standing away from the rest of them, clinging to each other. Isaiah didn't touch them.

'So,' said Macey, trying to sound cool, 'we may have to add another coat of paint down there.' It didn't come out cool; it came out trembly.

'My grandma says living here is like war,' said Venita. 'You watch TV news? I love TV news. They show wars all over the world. They should just set cameras on this corner. Snipers, drive-bys, gang shootings. You got drug ODs and crack crazies, and you got kids their moms never home and they burn theirselves in spaghetti water.' She grinned at Macey. 'But not me. Not my family. And not the kids in this day care. And now I been in a fire, and I won. They can't burn me.' Venita was laughing. She put her hand on

Macey's shoulder. 'Now you, on the other hand, you burned. Thought you were a goner.'

'Me?' Macey realized they were staring at her – Lindsay and Grace and Austin, the firemen, a gathering crowd – and Venita said gently, 'You know a hairdresser you can hit tonight, Mace? 'Cause you look funny with an Afro.'

Macey touched her head.

Her hair, her wonderful, precious hair she was so proud of; its colour and highlights, its sheen and body, all the things they told you shampoo was supposed to give you, but Macey just had – there was nothing left.

Two or three inches of shag stank and broke off when she pressed her palm against it. *She had no hair*.

Macey was afraid she was going to start crying. It was only hair, she couldn't cry, she could not make a scene, it was hair.

'I put out your fire,' said Austin.

Venita said, 'Naw, you ain't put out her fire, Texas. She still got sparks for you.'

'Stop it, Venita. Don't listen to her, Aus. She's making that up.'

Austin said, 'Well, anyway, it was my T-shirt I used to smother the flames that were burning you.'

'Thank you,' she said. So that was why he was bare-chested and she was holding a T-shirt to her chest like a teddy bear.

Reverend Warren, the adult painters, the baking crew from the kitchen and finally Graff came running around the church.

What took them so long? Macey wondered.

Or maybe it wasn't long. Maybe the whole event had lasted only the time it would take to leave the half-court gym, go back through the kitchen, up through the offices, unlock the parking gate, circle the church property – to find seven kids laughing because they were fine, and the eighth pretending she didn't care that her hair was burned off and she was left with a piece of sooty carpet up there.

'What'd you do, Graff,' said Austin, 'go out for hamburgers and shakes?'

Graff checked them feverishly, patting them down like suspects in a hijacking. 'Oh, my God,' said Graff, 'what are your parents going to say to me?'

Nobody even had a blister, and only Macey was coughing a little.

'Take you to the hospital for observation,' said the paramedic.

'No, no,' said Macey quickly, 'I'm fine. But – but how come I'm the only one who got burned?'

'Sparks, probably,' said a fireman. 'Your hair flying out behind you when you ran. You were tinder. Everybody else was wearing a baseball cap or their hair is close to their head. You're lucky the other kid put out the fire or you wouldn't have a face left.'

'Oh, my God,' said Graff again. 'Your parents—'

'Let's not tell the parents,' said Austin. 'This seems like a good thing to omit.'

Lindsay was recovering. She had her voice back. 'I can't believe you told me not to bring my mobile phone, Graff! I'll never listen to you again!' She turned to the firemen. 'Did somebody want us dead? Were they after us?'

'Doubt if anybody knew you were here,' said one fireman. 'Or cared. It was arson, though. Witnesses across the street saw the guy do it. 'Course, they didn't go after him. Can't give us a description, except he's black. Probably the same guy who hit two other churches in town, and the old temple. Nobody uses the temple any more, but that just makes it a better target.'

We were a target, thought Macey.

'We could skip the details when we talk to the parents, Austin,' agreed Graff, 'if Macey still had hair on her head. But she's going home in a skull.'

'A skull!' shrieked Macey. 'Where's a mirror? How bad is this?'

'You'll look fine,' Venita consoled her. 'You get one of those cute little haircuts, like a buzz for the marines. Razor-cut a design in it.'

Macey closed her eyes and set her jaw against sobbing. Lindsay and Grace immediately wrapped their arms around her and ordered Graff to bring the van around.

Austin said, 'No, no, we can't leave. The fire is out. There's going to be a lot of cleanup. We're here, and we can help.'

'Austin, don't be a jerk!' said Grace. 'We nearly got killed!' She turned to Reverend Warren and said, 'How could you have the exit locked? That is the stupidest thing I ever heard of! What do you think an exit door is for, anyway?'

'Grace, don't be rude,' said Macey, and Grace said, 'Mace. We nearly *died* and you are worried about *rude?*'

Reverend Warren said softly, 'Thank you, Austin,

but the four of you are more responsibility than I can handle right now. If we're sure that everyone is just shaken up and not hurt, I'm going to send you on home.' He said to Grace, 'You are right. Chaining the bulkhead doors was stupid. But somebody broke in a few months ago when we had the children here, and he stabbed a nine-year-old. The property committee was more scared of who could break in than they were of fire.'

Macey forgot her hair.

What was hair?

A nine-year-old stabbed in a Sunday school room. An arsonist who had hit two other churches and a temple. *Hell itself breathes out Contagion to this world.*

Venita walked Macey a few feet away from the others. 'Don't cry,' she said. 'Your hair will grow back.' Venita tilted her head and gave Macey a mischievous grin. 'And one nice thing.'

'Oh, sure,' said Macey.

'Texas is real proud of saving you,' said Venita. 'He's your man, whether him and you want it or not.'

In the van, they all agreed to play this down. It just didn't seem like the kind of publicity needed by Saturday Group or the community service programme. And how could it help Good Shepherd or the sister arrangement between the churches?

'Macey's hair is a problem,' Grace pointed out. 'She's not invisible. The rest of us don't have proof of fire, but she sure does.'

Macey peered between the two front seats to catch a

glimpse of herself in the rearview mirror. It was too narrow to show much.

'I can just say there was a minor fire in the hall,' said Macey, 'and I was wearing my hair loose, and like a jerk, I went over to see if I could put it out, instead of sensibly running away like everybody else. Then I can move right on to how Austin saved me with his T-shirt.'

She did not know for sure why the others wanted to fake what had happened, but she knew why she wanted to. Everything had happened too fast; fire and talk and thought and people had spattered her like paint. She was still caught in the horrible moment when her hair smoked and a padlock sealed them in. She wanted to think about Venita and Shakespeare and broken crayons and Sunday school rooms where all the yellow paint in the world would not protect a nine-year-old.

She wanted to turn this over in her mind, and she wanted to do this alone. Not with Mom or Dad. Not with Nana or Papa. Never had she yearned for the solitude of her own mind. Now she needed it.

As they'd climbed into the van, Chamique had silently handed Macey a paper plate stacked with Dorothy Edna's cinnamon-icing sticky buns. Neatly sandwiched in the layers of plastic wrap were enough paper napkins to go around. Macey passed the buns. They were scrumptious. She would save one for Nana to try to duplicate.

'Oh, no!' said Grace suddenly. 'We didn't give them the beanbag chairs and the crayon can.'

Macey was glad. She had met only four kids from the

church, and none of the sixes who would play in the room of gold, but she wanted something else for them.

We give Good Shepherd our old supplies and our old furniture, she thought, picking up a ruined crayon. I thought that was kind. But maybe it isn't. Maybe it's saying: you don't deserve anything as good as we have. You can have our leftovers. But you can't have anything new and just right.

Austin smiled at her with cinnamon-icing lips and patted the seat next to him.

'And my face,' she said to him very softly when they were next to each other, and now she did begin to cry. 'Oh, Aus, if it weren't for you, if you hadn't been there, my face would be burned.'

He put his arm around her and hauled her in close, resting his cheek against her crinkly hair, while Lindsay and Grace made annoying little coos of observation.

Venita was right. One nice thing.

Austin.

The instant Graff pulled up at the church, Lindsay was out of the van, unlocking her own car and pulling out her phone. 'I'm calling my hairdresser,' she said to Macey. 'We'll drive straight over.' Into the phone she said, 'Sasha, we have a hair emergency. You must fit us in.'

'Let's all go,' said Austin.

Macey did not know how she felt about having a party during the shaving of her head.

'Sasha will take you,' said Lindsay, handing Macey the phone. 'Now get your fibs ready, call your mother,

43

and yes, of course everybody can go. We'll stop to buy a disposable camera first.'

'No!' shrieked Macey. She turned to Grace for support, but Grace whispered, 'If we'd had a camera in the van, you'd have a picture of yourself in Austin's arms.'

That was tempting, and Macey was sorry such a picture did not exist, but she certainly didn't want any pictures of herself until she knew what she looked like. It was unfair that everybody could inspect the hair emergency except Macey herself.

The hairdresser was able to save about an inch and a half of hair. It didn't stick up, like a buzz, but lay rather softly. It was not the look that was weird – although each glance in a mirror was startling – but the weight. Her head was lighter. She felt as if her skull showed, a feeling akin to going around without a bra.

The smell could not be cut off.

Even though Sasha insisted that Macey looked elegant and trendy; even though Austin said he liked it that way; even though her mother and father spent Saturday evening insisting that every bit of burned hair was gone; even though Nana and Papa drove over to make sure their darling granddaughter was really all right; and even though they too said they could not smell fire on her head, the burning was with her through the night.

Her hair had gone up in smoke.

How incredible, how lucky, that they themselves had not.

Austin dreamed that night of fire.

In his dream, a little kid who loved hiding places fell

asleep inside bleached bones of driftwood. Gasoline poured down and drenched the child, and Austin could see the face as the child burned, and it was somebody he knew, and Austin woke up sick and shivering, blankets on the floor, window open to a cold April dawn.

It's only a dream, he said to himself. Nobody died inside the bonfire. Nobody even got a blister in the Good Shepherd fire.

He couldn't get warm.

He couldn't go back to sleep.

He lay flat on his back and reviewed the minute, or eternity, they had spent in the triangular prison beneath the chained exit. Crouched between Chamique and Macey, knowing the next smoke-laden breath would kill him, he had had only one syllable in his head.

No.

Not a screaming *No no no no no don't do this to me!*

A simple quiet refusal.

No.

This was not his destiny. He was rich and smart and attractive and . . . white.

He had actually had that thought. It's OK for them, he had thought, but this isn't supposed to happen to me.

The evil of his final thought – what would have been his final thought if the firemen had not been so quick – this evil stayed awake in him, until eventually he had to get up and shower again; try the hot water cure for sin.

Austin had not telephoned his parents to tell about the fire, and he made light of it to his grandparents.

'Smoke, mostly,' he said, shrugging.

They shook their heads. 'That's the problem with this community service programme,' Henry Fent said. 'It's poorly supervised, with no real goals.'

There had been a wonderful goal – making the day care rooms bright and cheerful for a hundred little kids who were hopping up and down because they needed to go to the bathroom so bad. But arguing with Grandfather never got Austin anywhere.

Now he stared into his soul, the one that thought he deserved better than Venita and Davonn and Chamique and Isaiah, and that didn't get him anywhere either.

At school, Macey was a celebrity.

People came over and exclaimed over her close call, and how lucky she was to be alive, and how glad they were she had not burned to a crisp. Boys, girls, teachers and parents said carefully, 'And I love your hair like that.'

'It's enough to make a person suspicious,' said Macey to Austin.

'What do you mean?'

'Too many compliments. I feel as if I'm going around with my head on a spike for people to stare at.'

Austin was laughing. 'It's a nice head.'

'It still smells of burn.'

'No, it doesn't. You just remember burning. I do too. I dream it at night. In my dream, the flames aren't on your head, they're around my feet, and when I try to step out, the fire climbs into my hands and my hands burn off.'

'Nice,' said Macey.

'Don't suggest a counsellor. I'll be fine in a minute.'

'On Sunday, I wrote to Venita, care of Reverend Warren at Good Shepherd, because I didn't know her last name, let alone her address.'

'Yeah? She write back?'

'Right away. She said it's mostly smoke damage and since they're painting anyway, they're not really in a worse position. The problem is after-school care. Until it's painted, which was supposed to be over the weekend, they have a hundred little kids with nowhere to go.' Macey showed Austin the letter. 'In my letter, I told Venita I'd rather e-mail, so I gave her my e-mail address, and you know what she said in her letter?'

'What?'

'She said they don't have any computers at her high school. Do you believe that?'

She was actually asking him this, so he said, 'Yes, I believe it. It's an inner-city school. They're way behind on everything. Didn't you hear her say they couldn't even read American literature this year because they didn't have classroom copies of the books?'

'Yes, but I didn't believe her.'

'Well, they don't have computers.'

'This is Connecticut,' protested Macey.

Austin was not now and never had been interested in Connecticut. And yet it amazed him that Macey could think every town in the entire state was a duplicate of her own immensely wealthy town.

He said, 'I like your new haircut just fine, but I thought you might like coverage.' He handed over a baseball cap with the logo of the UConn Huskies basketball team. He'd bought it yesterday, wondering if he was supposed to wrap it, or if that would make it too important. Macey gave the cap a smile and put it on frontward, yanking it low. Austin lifted the bill of the cap a little to see her better.

He had to stoop down to do it, and when their eyes met, Austin's heart felt like a rowboat loose in the sea.

'I saved the T-shirt,' she said. She put both her hands flat on the dark grey tee he was wearing. He could feel her hands. He could feel all ten fingers and her palms. 'I hung it in Papa and Nana's back porch. I made them swear not to throw it out. Nana thinks salt air will take away the smell.'

'Nothing will take away the burn holes,' he said. He was getting a headache from how hard his heart was pounding. No fair.

By late afternoon, Macey's voice was warmed up and ready to use. She needed two hours of phone conversation.

Lindsay had got heavily into e-mail and preferred to keyboard back and forth. Macey did not object to e-mail, but since it did not include the sound of her own voice, it would never be number one. So she called Grace. Grace's finest asset was that she could hold a phone for two hours and not say anything except, 'And then what happened?'

'It's me,' announced Macey. 'Forget all other topics. We have a big one. I'm in love with Aus.'

'That's perfect. The boy across the street. And he's such a cutie.'

The number of people with that opinion was rising.

Grace said, 'Tell me everything about Aus. How come he's here, how long will he stay, how much time do we have to work with, can you rope him and tie him down before he leaves?'

'Stop it, Grace. I'm not going to rope him,' said Macey indignantly. 'There will be no tying down.'

'We'll do it delicately. He'll hardly notice. He'll think he's in charge.'

'Grace! Nobody's in charge! It isn't that kind of a thing.'

'It's a crush. Somebody always has to be in charge with a crush. You can't just let it lie there. First give me the details on his family.'

'I don't have any.'

'Sic your grandmother on his grandmother.'

'Nana tried. She got nothing.'

'Whoa. Hard case. I could place demands. Aus and I will be in the media centre tomorrow for English class and I can sit next to him and say, '"So why are you here, Aus?"'

'Don't even think about it, Grace. But don't you love that syllabus – Aus? If you didn't know it came from Austin, you'd think it was peculiar, but since you do know, it's so cute.'

They settled into a discussion of Austin's mind, body and soul, and the various ways in which these were cute.

On Friday, Macey had a rare study period, but so many people were asking about her hair that she got a media centre pass. In the media centre there were so many people who hadn't seen her hair yet that she hid in a carrel with a computer.

She clicked Netscape and checked her mail, but there was none. She sloshed around the Internet. It had never occurred to her to look up anything local. Who cared? She was local already. Now she tried to find a hook, a way into whatever sources there were for her history project, and up came the town newspaper. Cool.

A few minutes on that site and she discovered the newspaper had its index online. She entered 'fires'.

There, in chronological order, were the fires reporters had covered since the newspaper was founded in 1924. They were listed by date, and next to the date was the address of the fire, and next to that the issue, page and column of the newspaper article. Wow, thought Macey, with the shiver of awe she often felt when she was using the Net.

December 4, 1959 . . . Shell Road . . .

It was as easy as that.

She could read about the barn fire.

But not, of course, on the Net. It was too cruel. You could look stuff up and find out it existed. But it didn't exist on the Net. And it didn't exist in the school media centre. To read the article, she'd have to go to the town library and find the right microfilm. How annoying.

Oh, well, at least her first hairless week was over.

Macey spent a while in the girls' room, admiring her cap from various angles. She was not in fact interested in college basketball, and whether UConn got to the Final Four or died early in the season meant zero to Macey Clare.

But this was a gift from Austin. The first present she had got from a boy since her last boy-girl birthday party, in second grade. Now she had an Austin clothing collection. T-shirt and cap.

Macey took her short cuts to Nana and Papa's, hoping to cross paths with Aus, but she didn't. It was a cloudy day, the kind where the entire sky is a slab of slate, lowering to crush your spirits. The swamp was ugly, and rain began just as she reached the road.

She could not find the old feeling of safely through another week. She was safe. A boy liked her, her hair would grow out. But in the swamp, under the bleak sky, she remembered the nine-year-old. The arson. Even the ruined crayons.

Nana and Papa fussed over her. They were annoyed with Mom and Dad for not taking earlier trains home this week. When your daughter had been burned in a fire in a slum church basement, you should have the parental concern to be home for dinner.

Macey had not wanted Mom and Dad home early. She liked routine, not change.

Papa touched her shorn hair. It was so short he couldn't wrap a curl around his plump finger. 'When I think what could have happened to you in that church! These people are so careless. They don't have any concern for their very own buildings.'

Since Macey had not admitted that it was arson, her grandfather's guess was fair enough. But if she explained the arson, he would say it was careless to leave cans of oil paint open, and turpentine open, and rags lying around, and really, really careless to open the side door, and beyond careless right into criminal to have chained the exit.

She had to defend Good Shepherd.

The church the Maceys attended was a huge, gaunt pile of stones, as if somebody had broken off a chunk of English cathedral and dropped it in green grass. It replaced a white wooden church that had burned on Christmas Eve 1892, when the choir set their candles down on piles of sheet music. 'Our church burned down,' Macey pointed out, 'a hundred years ago when the choir was careless.'

Papa dismissed this comparison with an irritated wave. 'You will not participate in Saturday Group again.'

Macey did not care for Papa's dictating mode. 'Well, we'll see, but I do want to go back to Good Shepherd. Even though Reverend Warren said we were too much responsibility for him, Austin and I thought we could—'

'Reverend Warren is right,' said Papa.

'Why on earth would you want to go back, anyway?' said Nana.

'I liked Venita. You know that special way you feel when a friendship is coming through? Not the slow kind of friendship, where you know somebody all your life, and you sit near each other and the years pass. The fast kind of friendship, where it's just there, and it's a privilege. And Venita—'

'Out of the question,' said Papa. 'Even your parents will back us up on this. You will never go near that city again.'

4

Saturday morning, the Clare family had an actual cooked breakfast. Macey would have to tell Nana and Papa. A meal with all three of them sitting at the same table, and the ingredients were hot and did not come from a fast-food restaurant. Macey whisked out china plates just in time to catch the food as it came off the skillet.

Toast, bacon, scrambled eggs, orange juice and potato chips.

'Stop that, Alec,' said Mom. 'Put away those potato chips.'

'If we were at the diner, I'd have home-fried potatoes,' he defended himself. 'It's practically the same.'

'You're not at the diner. Potato chips are junk food. Stop it.'

'I like potato chips.' He crunched.

Macey would omit the potato chips from the breakfast menu she told Nana and Papa. She was so happy to be sitting down with her parents. They muddled around the house in the comfy way of Saturday morning. Dad had another cup of coffee. Mom did a crossword and Dad squinted at the sports page.

'You know,' said Macey, 'Venita said they don't have computers in their high school. None at all.'

'That's a shame,' said her father. 'I think I'll go for a run. Want to run with me, Mace?' He stretched hugely and yawned and sprawled on the couch, not like a man about to go for a run.

'No, thanks, Dad. Mom? Do you think that giving people old and crummy stuff is the right thing to do, if they don't have anything at all, or do you think everybody ought to have new stuff?'

'Not everybody can afford new,' said her mother. 'And it's good to make use of old things that still have some life in them. That reminds me, I cannot postpone putting together the recycling stuff another day. Want to help, Alec?' She trekked slowly to the back porch, hoping Dad would offer to pile and bind and count. Dad lay low.

From the porch, Mom's giggle was clear and silly. 'Macey, you saved your marshmallow stick? Now I know the family desire to fill up back porches has reached the ultimate.'

Macey ran to save her stick. They honoured each other's junk piles, but you never knew what might get tossed when somebody was in a cleaning mood.

'What's special about it?' said Mom.

Austin carved it for me, Macey thought. It has his fingerprints on it. We both ate half of a perfectly toasted marshmallow, like a bride and groom sharing the first piece of wedding cake.

Macey had a shelf in her mind where she stored romantic events that had not happened. She knew perfectly well they had not eaten the marshmallow like a bride and groom. She'd had some, and then Austin had looked down and seen there was some left, so he'd eaten it. But of course, were she to grow up and marry Austin (which, now that he had given her a cap, seemed entirely possible) she would tell their children a long romantic story about that first marshmallow.

Children, she would say, the night before your father saved me from the fire . . .

How strange she felt around Austin: this lifelong acquaintance she did not know well, this neighbour who had saved her life, this cutie.

You got a crush on that boy? That one named for Texas?

'Nothing special,' she said to her mother. 'It's just a stick. By the way, Mom, when the Demitroffs' barn burned down, back in 1959, was somebody living in it or not?'

'It's so upsetting when you keep bringing up fire, Macey,' said her mother. 'Did you tell us everything there is to tell about getting your hair burned?'

'Now that I've felt fire, I'm interested in fire.' The word *fire* wasn't quite right. It was arson that interested her. But she hadn't told her parents about any arson. 'I'm doing it for my history paper.'

'Oh, Mace,' said her mother. 'You're going to have to put so many hours into this project. At least choose a topic that matters.'

'I'll ask Mrs Johnson about other topics,' Macey said. She might, too, although she'd be asking about topics for Austin. She was staying with the fire. 'But I still want to know. Did anybody live in that barn? In 1959?'

'My science teacher. Mr Sibley.'

'There *was* an apartment then?' said Macey.

'Oh, yes, it was such a sweet place. Everybody oohed and ahhed when they saw it. Of course, I never saw it when Mr Sibley was living there, but most years it was rented to a new teacher, and I'd bring a plate of Mother's cookies or a casserole and say hi and welcome to the neighbourhood, and I'd wander around and inspect the apartment.'

'But you didn't bring cookies to Mr Sibley?' said Macey.

There was a slight pause. 'I don't remember,' her mother said.

But you do remember, thought Macey. You remember you were never inside when Mr Sibley lived there.

Until now, Macey had forgotten the other pause, the faint pause before her grandparents answered questions about that old fire, and once more, the old fire prickled at her.

'Didn't you tell me, Cordelia,' said Dad, 'that that teacher got out in time because somebody on the other side of the creek saw flames and called the fire department?'

'Yes, that's right.'

At Good Shepherd, we got out in time because a fire truck just happened to be driving past as the flames took hold. We got out in time because we pounded and screamed loud enough that the firemen heard us and because they had the right tool to break the chain.

Had a guardian angel been at Good Shepherd? Directing traffic to save the eight of them? But a true guardian angel would have prevented the fire in the first place. And any guardian angel would have come to save the nine-year-old.

'Alec,' said her mother, 'Ginger Framm wants us to go with them on a house and garden tour.'

Macey could not tell if her mother was changing the subject or if her mother had not even noticed the subject.

'I hate house and garden tours,' moaned Dad. Dad didn't want tickets to anything, ever. When he was home, he was home. He liked to fool around on the computer, rent movies, maybe wash the car. But leaving the property for any reason other than life-support purchases was unfair torture for a man who had worked so hard all week.

'I know, but Ginger has to sell ten tickets.'

'Let's buy the tickets and not go,' said Dad.

Ginger Framm was Mom's lifelong best friend.

'Were you best friends with Mrs Framm back in 1959 too, Mom?'

'Oh, yes, Ginger and I have been best friends from kindergarten.'

Macey loved that. She and Grace had been best friends since first grade, and Lindsay had moved here when they were in fourth. She loved thinking of friendships lasting a lifetime.

I'm lucky I even *have* a lifetime, she thought.

She could smell smoke in her hair as strongly as if the fire still burned.

Austin's Grandfather's rowing machine was in the formal living room, a location Grandmother hated and had been complaining about for years. It faced towards the ocean so Grandfather could actually see the water as he rowed, as if he were out on it. When he did go out on the ocean, of course, he used his powerboat, and if he had to row, he would feel he had failed.

Austin had discovered that if he shifted a little armchair that was completely useless anyway, and tied the curtains back tighter than Grandmother liked them, and then gave the rowing machine a half turn, he could row watching the Macey house.

He was on the floor, however, and could see only the roof. He didn't want to admit he was watching for Macey's arrival, so when Grandfather asked why he'd turned the rowing machine, he said, 'It slipped,' which was totally stupid, because it weighed a jillion pounds and the floor was flat.

Grandfather said, 'Oh,' and sat in front of his telescope looking at a flock of mergansers in the cove, telling Austin that somebody at the Audubon Society claimed to have seen a loon there yesterday.

Austin felt he qualified.

By the end of his workout, however, he rounded up enough courage to walk across the street to the Maceys' to see if Macey was around. He had just hit the Maceys' back porch when he realized that in his condition, a shower would definitely have been in order.

'Hi, Austin,' said Macey's grandfather. 'She isn't here.'

Austin wanted to jump in the ocean and go live with the ducks. He could not stand it that Macey's grandfather knew why he was coming. So he said, 'I know. I just wondered if I could walk the dogs. Get a little exercise.'

Macey's grandfather looked at the sweat-soaked tracksuit Austin was wearing and said, 'Exercise is good, Aus, and you just feel free to go on doing my share.'

Moose could have run ten miles; it was Aus who had been rowing for an hour and couldn't walk faster or farther than Zipper. When he got back, Mrs Macey was melting chocolate. 'What are you going to make?' he wanted to know.

Macey's grandmother grinned at him. She was this fat old woman who had the cutest grin in the world. 'Lucky Devil's Cake,' she told him. 'As in ooooh, you lucky devil, you! You're getting the world's best chocolate cake.'

Austin laughed. 'Can I help, Mrs Macey?'

'Wash your hands. Wear that apron.'

Austin had never had an apron on. It was a rather pleasant feeling, like turning the computer on; he was ready.

He measured. He sifted. He added. He poured. He stirred. He got the bowl to lick. 'Wow,' he said to Macey's grandmother, 'why even bake it? Just pour it in a glass and drink it.'

She smiled, poured him a glass of cake and sent him home.

Macey had extra money, always a nice thing, so Saturday afternoon, she and Lindsay and Grace went shopping. Lindsay shared her car with her older brother and sister, and Saturdays she was last in line for the car, so Grace's mother dropped them off. They were limited to the streets within walking distance, and these were mainly shops they couldn't afford. But that was the best kind of shop for browsing.

They tried on clothes and shoes. They examined spring fashions and new bathing suit lines. They studied new lipstick colours. They deliberated among several new CDs, but Lindsay and Grace were so opposed to Macey's favourite rock bands that she didn't buy anything.

'So the Aus collection,' said Lindsay, 'consists of a twig, a T-shirt with holes in it and a cap for a team you don't care about.'

'The Aus collection,' said Macey with dignity, 'is a remarkable gathering of treasures of which you can only be jealous.'

They paused among scarves and accessories.

'This is the first time we've gone shopping without getting a hair ornament for you, Mace,' said Grace. When they were little, they had loved having rhyming names. Grace/Mace never failed to knock them down laughing. 'You now have the world's largest useless scrunchie, ribbon and hairslide collection,' Grace informed her.

'It's true,' said Macey, touching her short hair. 'But I'm going to grow it out, so in another five years or so I can use scrunchies again.' Five years. She would be in college. Halfway through college. This was an incredible thought. She said, 'You know, I keep thinking about Venita and Chamique.'

'You're kidding,' said Grace. 'I plan never to think of

them or that place again. That was the scariest day of my life.'

'The fire was the scariest,' agreed Macey, 'but I meant Venita. I can't get over how she was quoting Shakespeare. I don't have any Shakespeare by memory. I couldn't have launched into *Hamlet* even though we read it last year.'

'Shakespeare?' repeated Lindsay, laughing. 'Macey, what are you talking about? Venita? The one with all the braids? Quoting Shakespeare? Give me a break, Mace.'

Macey had forgotten that Lindsay and Grace had been in another room, busily not talking to Chamique, while a radio filled the silence. 'Well, Venita and Isaiah knew Shakespeare better than I do, and I didn't expect that.'

''Cause you're racist,' said Grace. 'We're all racist. Look at this darling top! Do you love this little vest thing or what? What is it, anyway?'

They took turns trying it on. It was a garment with no name or purpose, and they ended up giggling steadily, unable to imagine where you would wear this thing with one sleeve, half a front, and great colours for which you would have paid several hundred dollars. Lindsay bought a sweater instead.

Grace's mother picked them up, but Macey decided to walk home. She felt all cramped in the knees at the end of a day if she hadn't swung her stride to its limit.

She cut through a side street, and there was the gift shop that Mom's friend Mrs Framm had opened several years ago. Mrs Framm was another one of these people

61

who thought Macey was perfect, and it was always worthwhile to drop in on Mrs Framm so she could tell Macey again how perfect she was.

The shop's speciality was lamp shades. Her shades were pleated and laced and stencilled and painted and gilded and trimmed. Macey tried to imagine a life so boring that you got excited about the edges of your lamp shades.

'Macey!' said Mrs. Framm, hugging and admiring. 'Macey, darling, I *love* the slinky haircut. My dear, you are so au courant! Wherever did you find the courage to cut off your magnificent hair?'

Mom hasn't told her about the fire, thought Macey.

Did they have better things to talk about? Did they talk about the house and garden tour instead of me?

She felt two years old, wanting to be the centre of her mother's universe, the sole subject of her mother's conversation. 'I got caught in a teensy silly accidental fire. I let my hair hang down where I shouldn't have.'

'Oh, no. Over the burner on the stove, or something?' cried Mrs Framm.

'Exactly.'

'My darling, thank God you are all right!'

They talked about the struggle to sell house and garden tour tickets, and Macey said, 'Mrs Framm, do you remember your seventh-grade science teacher?'

'I was in boarding school in seventh grade. Why would you want to know about my boarding-school teachers?'

'Seventh grade? I thought boarding schools started in ninth.'

'Mostly they do. I started early.'

''Weren't you homesick and lonely? Wasn't it awful?'

'It was ghastly. Promise me you'll never do it to your daughter.'

'I promise.'

'You were probably thinking of your mother's seventh-grade science teacher. Mr Sibley.' Mrs Framm swayed and shook her head and rolled her eyes. She always did this, however, so it didn't mean much. 'What a thing that was. That was the whole reason I was sent to boarding school.'

A fire? thought Macey. She was sent to boarding school because of a fire?

Macey tasted her own fire, the horror of being suffocated. She had not known when cloth was pushed down over her head and eyes and ears and nose that there was a reason. She had known only that she was helpless and blind and running out of oxygen. She had fought and tried to scream, but part of the T-shirt got in her mouth and she'd choked on cotton and smoke.

If she'd been responsible for saving Aus, could she have thought and acted as fast as he had?

'You see,' said Ginger Framm, 'my parents would have died before letting me sit in a classroom run by a Negro.'

Macey's jaw fell open. Mrs Framm said, 'Don't look at me like that. You said *Negro* then, you didn't say *African American* or *black*. And you considered yourself very civilized for not using a worse word. Anyway, Mr Sibley was the first Negro teacher in town. The school system had never had a coloured teacher before.'

Why hadn't her mother said so? It was not something you could forget. If you remembered Mr Sibley at all, you'd remember that.

Austin's grandmother 'vaguely' remembered the barn fire. And Nana had said, Every flame the same as the next.

The first black teacher in town? Living in the apartment over the stable down the street? And it burned down? And they couldn't remember?

Macey did not believe it was possible to forget a fire. She would remember the cold filth of the cement steps they had not been able to climb. The ribbed steel of the bulkhead door under her searching fingers. The pressure of Venita's and Austin's bodies against hers.

She would remember the shade of yellow in her Sunday school room for the sixes; she would remember *Hamlet*.

Suppose it was arson, she thought, that fire in 1959. Then . . . *who started it?*

'Your parents sent you to boarding school,' she repeated. Her hands were trembling. She could feel the lightness of her hair.

Mrs Framm was smiling. 'Otherwise, a Negro would have been telling me what to learn, as if he knew something, like a regular person.'

Macey's feet kept balance, but her mind tipped. She wanted to reach out for support, but this was the kind of shop with thousands of tiny breakables, so if you backed up wrong or swung your purse too wide, some little crystal thing died. 'I can't believe you're saying this.' She looked around to make sure there were no customers listening.

Mrs Framm shrugged. 'Mace, honey, that was four decades ago. Times change. But back then, as far as people in this town were concerned, Negroes weren't quite people. They were not equal. And even though you sang in church about "O Brother Man," coloured people came in a separate category, and they weren't your brother, unless they were safely in Africa or some distant state like Mississippi. Then they could be your brother.'

They're still in a separate category, thought Macey. We have books. They have photocopies. We have computers. They have toilets without lids.

Mrs Framm nudged her glasses up her nose and examined the lamp shades around her. 'But they could not be your neighbour. Absolutely, positively not your neighbour. So I got sent to boarding school, to keep me safe.'

While Mr Sibley, not so safe, slept in a barn that burned.

The only people likely to start a fire to drive somebody out of the neighbourhood were people who lived in the neighbourhood. And who had lived on Shell Road in December 1959?

Macey beat this thought down as if she were putting out a fire on her head.

Two women came into the shop in search of wedding gifts, live customers ready to spend, and Macey was in the way. She walked to her parents' house, every thought a spark. The fire was not on her head this time, but in it.

It smouldered and smoked, and whenever she tried to stop thinking of 1959, she felt herself inside Austin's bad dream, with fire climbing into her hands.

Austin was desperately sorry they had decided to lie about the fire.

Well, not lie, really. Just not tell.

His need to talk filled his grandparents' house like smoke itself, and finally he went up to his bedroom to be alone and he called home. Mom answered. She chatted in the high-pitched casual way she had when everything was miserable and wrong. He listened to her for a while and then he said, 'Grandfather finished teaching me to drive, Mom.'

He could drive now, had passed the test, was the possessor of a driver's licence. But not in Illinois, where he had been born and had spent his entire life. It was a Connecticut driver's licence. There was something solemn and terrible about that – his first official ID from the wrong state.

'Oh,' said his mother.

He pulled the cord of the blinds and closed them all the way and then he pulled again and opened them. But she didn't say more about her only son learning to drive.

'Mom, Macey is interested in that old barn fire in 1959. Do you remember it?'

'I was in second grade,' she said. 'I think Macey's mother was very upset by it. Cordelia used to babysit for me, did you know that? We never got to be friends. Five years apart is too many.'

His mother had not asked how he was doing, or what he was doing, or how school was, or if he needed clothes. 'Mom,' he said, trying not to sound desperate, 'how are you and Dad getting along? What have you decided?'

There was a long, irritated sigh, as if it were none of his business; as if she were getting pretty tired of this interference in her private life. 'Nothing has changed, Austin. Your father is working evenings, so he's asleep when I'm at work and so forth. We're in different bedrooms and we hardly see each other. It isn't a life. I don't know what it is.'

'Is it a divorce?' he said. Dad was an emergency-room doctor. He came home so tired he'd just crash.

Mom wanted more life. She wanted parties and movies and tickets and shows and travel and hobbies, and Dad just wanted a nap.

'What do you want it to be?' she snapped.

'It's your call, Mom. I just want to know what's going on.'

'I don't know what's going on.'

He hung up on her.

He had never done that, and the shock of it was like a slap.

His parents didn't know about his fires, the one at Good Shepherd or the one raging in him for Macey.

I should go home, he thought. Home to Chicago. We're having a triple divorce here: mine, Mom's and Dad's. Soon we'll have three houses where there used to be one. I should at least be there to help pack, or wave goodbye, or write down their phone numbers, or something.

He began to understand why people talked to God. You didn't need to give half so much background or play as many games.

Every morning going into New York on the train, Macey's father read two newspapers, and every evening coming home, he read a book. He favoured six- or eight-hundred-page books that would keep him going for weeks.

'What's your book?' Macey asked that night. She and Dad were sprawled in front of the TV, while Mom was hypnotized by her computer. They'd lost the remote and didn't have the strength to get up and change the channel by hand to something they actually wanted to see. A nature show was on, and Macey listened to the familiar voice droning about zebras during a drought. She could narrate this herself. Soon the rains would come.

'I'm reading *The Fifties*. I grew up in the fifties, so I figured I knew everything, but it turns out I don't know anything.'

Macey was not normally fascinated by the 1950s, which seemed as remote as pyramids on the Nile, but she had been thinking of Mr Sibley, and she said, 'What was it like to be black in the fifties?'

'Bad. Segregation was still very harsh. Desegregation was just beginning, against great hostility. The action was in scary states like Mississippi and Alabama.'

'We weren't scary?' said Macey.

'No, in New England we were civilized,' said her father. 'In the Deep South, they were stoning children and arresting ministers and lynching people. Of course, nothing like that ever happened here,' said Dad, gesturing loosely towards the window and the six states of New England. 'I never saw segregation.'

'What do you mean?' said Macey, almost tempted to laugh. 'We're totally segregated. The firemen at Good Shepherd were stunned to see Aus and me and Lindsay and Grace. Nobody white lives there. Just like nobody black lives here.'

'Nonsense, Macey,' said her mother, who had been paying attention after all. 'It was in the paper just the other day that minority groups make up twelve per cent of our town's population.'

'Mom,' said Macey, exasperated. 'That's including the Japanese kids whose fathers run conglomerates in New York, the kids from India whose fathers are at the United Nations, and all the babies from South America that yuppies adopted.'

'They count,' said her mother.

'I'm talking about people like Mr Sibley or Venita. Ordinary black people who buy a house and stay.'

'No,' said her mother slowly. She looked tired, and Macey felt guilty about working her over. 'You're right, Mace. We're as segregated as the South ever was. We're just sly about it.'

The word *sly* filled the room, a syllable halfway between *lies* and *sleaze*.

Her father said, 'I read in the *New York Times* that

Harvard University came out with a report on segregation today. Connecticut and Mississippi have the same level of segregation. We're the worst states.'

We're the worst? thought Macey. She had been brought up to believe in the perfection of this, her home: every sugar maple tree, stone wall, church steeple and high tide was perfect.

'But we never had awful laws here. That was the South,' said her mother. 'The segregation today is an accident of wealth or lack of wealth.'

Her father was falling asleep. He slept in a neat, condensed way, his chin on his chest, his arms folded around him.

Macey picked up his book. Her eyes wandered down the chapter descriptions in the front. Thirty-six was about desegregation, which seemed like a lot of chapters to wait.

It began with Rosa Parks. It turned out that Rosa Parks got on the bus in 1955. Four years before Mr Sibley's fire. Mom had been seven. When the bus boycott in Montgomery, Alabama, began (the first thing in desegregation the whole country noticed), Martin Luther King Jr. had been twenty-six. In 1956, said the book, Martin Luther King's house was bombed. He had babies. They were home.

Macey closed the book.

Her mother was immersed in her computer screen. Her father had slid lower on the couch, deeper into sleep.

Macey could not imagine anybody closing a hand around an explosive.

Or could she?

She knew now what arson was. She knew how fire felt, and how smoke tasted. She stared at the dark shimmer of glass that faced the street. The Clares never closed their curtains. They were comfortable with the dark. But there was another kind of dark. The darkness of minds full of hate.

And Mr Sibley – what mind full of hate had he met? Macey read on.

A civil rights leader said to the young Reverend King, as he first began to lead, 'The Lord has laid his hands on you, and that is a dangerous thing.'

Macey imagined the hands of the Lord falling on her shoulders, touching her forehead, His voice saying, You must do this.

The chapter ended way too soon, Macey had hardly learned anything. The book went on to Marilyn Monroe. Macey could not believe it. How did they go from bombing a minister's house to a sex goddess?

Hands fell on her shoulder, and Macey almost screamed.

'Sorry,' said her father. 'I thought you knew me.'

'I was in the fifties,' said Macey. 'I thought you were the hands of the Lord.'

Macey had not read under the covers in years.

She didn't have to now. It would never cross her parents' minds to check whether her lights were out. But it felt safer under the covers, with the heat and weight of blankets tucking her in.

The story picked up in chapter forty-four.

Little Rock, Arkansas. No black child had ever been

in the same school with a white. Two thousand white children at Central High. Nine black children willing to be the first. The governor ordered the National Guard to the school to keep the nine children out.

Macey read that twice, to be sure. To keep nine children *out* of the building?

Yes, the state brought in its own army, whose soldiers said, We're here to keep the niggers out.

Macey hated having that word in the room with her. She put her finger over the word to clean up the page and read on.

Fifteen-year-old Elizabeth Eckford came to the school alone. Black and alone in a dress she had made herself for the new experience. 'Here she comes!' shouted the crowd. 'Here comes one of the niggers!'

Macey did not like crowds. She didn't like being squashed on to bleachers for a football game and she didn't like taking the subway at rush hour, pressed forward by a crowd that might shove her off the edge.

A crowd holding stones.

To throw.

At you.

Screaming: 'Go home, you black bitch!'

A Guardsman lifted his rifle – but not to protect Elizabeth. He pointed it at her. Bayonet and all, he pointed it at a fifteen-year-old girl. Someone yelled, 'Lynch her!' and the mob pressed closer.

Macey could not keep the book under the covers with her. She dropped it to the floor, and it fell facedown, pages splayed and bent, like what the crowd wanted to do to Elizabeth Eckford.

I'm fifteen, too, thought Macey. What if I sewed my own dress, and ironed it that morning, and prayed with my parents, and walked up to a school – a school! a perfectly ordinary school! – me and my skin, because I can't go without it – and hundreds of sweaty, angry, shouting people who think I'd be better off with a rope around my neck surrounded me?

I wouldn't be brave enough to stay in school after that.

I wouldn't care about school after that.

5

Grace said, 'No. Tell me it isn't true, Macey. You are not still taking your short cuts. Tell me you have grown up and you use pavements or, better yet, cars.'

'I am extremely grown-up, I am remarkably mature, and I trespass at every opportunity.'

'Is the barbed wire still there, or have you cut it down, rolled it up and made it easier on yourself?'

'It's somebody else's barbed wire, Grace, I'm not going to damage it. I'm not a vandal or a thief. I'm a simple trespasser.'

Grace moaned. 'Oh, for a driver's licence and a reasonably sane friend.'

They reached the barbed wire and Grace rolled her eyes, walked up and down the fence, discovered no way around, and let Macey hold the wires for her. 'Good thing I'm a size six,' said Grace. 'How do *you* fit through?'

'I happen to be a ten, thank you, not an eighteen.'

'We petites,' said Grace.

'Will end up dead with one more remark about size,' said Macey. They reached her board in the swamp, and Macey put her weight on it to test it.

It didn't bounce. There was somebody at the other end of the board.

For a heart-stopping second she was afraid, and then

she said, 'Oh, hi, Aus.' She wanted to fling herself on him. She stayed at her end of the board. Why had she picked today to invite Grace over to Nana and Papa's?

'Hey, Mace,' said Austin. And then, with less enthusiasm, 'Oh, hi, Grace.'

'Want me to leave?' whispered Grace.

'Like it wouldn't be too obvious if you turned around and went back through the barbed wire now,' whispered Macey.

From his end of the board, Austin said, 'There isn't a single living creature in this swamp. I've been here ten minutes and there's no bird, no squirrel, no frog.'

Ten minutes? thought Macey. Spent waiting for me, maybe?

He's your man whether him and you want it or not.

'Probably the end of the world, then, Aus,' said Grace. 'The great environmental shutdown has begun and you are there.'

Her grandmother and Venita and Grace agreed that Aus was a cutie. It wasn't the word Macey would choose. He was too solid for that; too stocky and a little short in the legs. He looked like the foundation for something. Macey's life, maybe.

'Listen,' said Grace. 'That sliding harmonica? A cardinal. That three-note whistle? Red-winged blackbird.'

'I'm not a naturalist,' admitted Austin. He held out a hand to Macey, as if the board were a high wire.

'Your grandfather keeps a telescope on a tripod aimed at the ocean,' Macey reminded him. 'You could start there. Watch ducks through the scope.'

75

Their hands touched. Austin took hers firmly and grinned at her, a grin that lifted his cheeks, resettled his hair and twinkled his eyes. Oh, wow, thought Macey. She was glad now that Grace was there; they could discuss that grin for days.

'I could,' said Austin. 'But one squint at a duck is enough for a lifetime.'

She giggled, which was an error. She began to tilt. Austin grabbed her arm. They flailed around, lost their balance together, yelled and fell off the board into the muck. Macey just wrecked her shoes, but Austin went down to his knees.

'I,' said Grace, 'will handle myself better, as befitting my name.' She walked neatly down the board, while Aus and Macey sloshed up on to the grass and sat down on the stones of the old barn to take off their shoes and socks.

'It's nice to be barefoot,' said Macey. 'Doesn't it make you think of summer and toenail polish and getting a tan?'

'No,' said Austin.

Macey wiggled her toes. Austin wiggled his. They had a little toe conversation, and it turned out that Austin could wave goodbye with his little toe. Macey had to move all her toes or none.

'Take off your shoes, Grace,' Austin invited her.

'I'm your chaperone,' said Grace. 'Chaperones keep their shoes on.'

Austin poured mud out of his sneakers and stuffed his wet socks inside them. 'This is that barn foundation you were talking about, isn't it, Macey?'

She nodded.

He said, 'I asked my mother what she remembered about the fire.'

Austin never referred to his parents. Macey remembered her assignments from Nana and Grace. But when she looked at Aus, his stocky frame meant for lifting and hauling, his wide face with its calm, wide expression, as if he could take more than most people, she knew she was not going to ask him. Whatever had happened was his property.

'She couldn't think of anything,' he said. 'She was too young.'

'Well, I found out some stuff. Get this. Not only was there a teacher living here, but he was the first black teacher ever hired in this town.'

'And the barn burned down around him?' asked Grace. 'I could draw a conclusion from that.'

'Me too,' said Macey. 'Neighbourhood legend, which I am unable to verify, is that it was arson and the guy was trapped inside. I'm going to find out. I'm going to do that for my history project.'

'Ugh,' said Grace. 'I hate stories like that. Pick something nice.'

'My feet are too cold to sit any longer,' said Austin, getting up.

Macey didn't want him to walk away; she wanted to live with him. 'Papa turned the water on,' she said, heading for their house. 'We can hose our shoes down.'

'In my part of town,' said Grace, 'we keep our shoes free of mud to start with.'

Macey scooped some mud off the bottom of her shoe and flung a little Grace's way. They had been good friends for a long time. Grace just laughed. She knew perfectly well that Macey would aim to miss.

Outside showers and spigots were turned off for the winter so pipes wouldn't freeze. April water, however, would certainly feel like ice. Macey and Austin carried their muddy shoes to the side of the house and held them under the faucet. It was hopping cold on their toes. They dried their bare feet on the grass and went inside, tossing shoes and socks on to the chaos of the porch.

Macey almost asked Aus about his collections, his junk and piles of stuff but stopped in time. You couldn't fit history into a suitcase. Poor Aus! she thought. For his sake, she spent a moment or two hating his parents for whatever they'd done wrong.

Grace whispered, 'Why don't I bail out and leave you two alone?'

'No, no, I invited you for dinner. Now I'll invite Aus, too, and Nana and Papa love dinner guests, and everybody will be happy, especially me.'

Inside the Macey kitchen, of course, Mr and Mrs Macey were in the middle of a serious project – a Martha Stewart recipe that listed not only food ingredients, but also the hardware store requirements, They had been working on this recipe since yesterday.

Austin loved how Mrs Macey got so happy with her own cooking, she had to smile at the sight of it.

'My mom gave up cooking,' said Austin.

'Poor dear,' said Nana, who felt so sorry for anybody who didn't love cooking. 'Don't you think a good hot dinner with a crisp salad and a yummy dessert, say silk chocolate pie in a crushed-cookie crust, would cheer her up?'

For the first time, Aus saw a resemblance between his grandmother and Macey's – the little hint that Mom wasn't conducting herself the way she'd been brought up. 'Sure, if you made it for her,' he said easily.

'No, no, the zest is in making it yourself, Austin. All the lovely little chores. The measuring, the mixing, the chopping, the toasting and then all the lovely waiting.'

But Macey and I, thought Austin, have parents who do not wait. Waiting is not lovely for them, it's a waste of time.

He wondered what kind of life he wanted, and he wondered, if he were there and knew what to do, whether he would paste his parents back together or let them go their separate ways.

Macey took a seat on a high counter stool, and Grace took another, so Austin did too, scootching to get comfortable just like they did. He was glad Grace was around. It softened his uncertainty to have two girls instead of one, although that was mathematically ridiculous: he should have been twice as anxious instead of half as anxious. They all three leaned on their elbows, accepting cups of hot chocolate with whipped cream. Austin curled his bare toes around the wooden footrest and listened to the elder Maceys chatter about nothing.

Between them, Austin's own grandparents chaired something like six committees. Tonight was committees.

And here at the Maceys', the world was food, had been food yesterday, would be food again tomorrow. Although his mother did not cook, and he could not think of her in a kitchen context, he wanted to call her. Tell her he was sorry for hanging up on her last week.

In order to keep track of the famous chefs whose techniques and styles ran this household, Nana and Papa had two televisions: one on the kitchen counter, with a tiny screen, and one across the room, with an immense screen. Austin picked up the remote, faced it to the large television and clicked around till he found the evening news.

'We don't watch that channel,' said Papa firmly. 'Connecticut news isn't news. They never cover anything but crime. Or nonsense, like who won the lottery and whether there's a fun time to be had visiting historic houses in Wethersfield.'

'If you really want news, Austin,' said Nana, 'and I don't, because it's dinnertime and why get upset about things you can't change, at least put on a New York station, where they'll have real news.'

Austin glanced down at the remote. The arrangement of buttons was different from his own remotes.

'See?' said Papa irritably. 'I'm right. Some kid has been shot and killed and we're going to have to look at it. I hate these shootings. I read the other day it's safer in Israel than New Haven.'

Austin clicked down a channel.

'*Austin, go back!*' said Macey. She hit his arm.

He stared at her.

She was not looking at him. She was leaning way

forward over the counter, staring at the wide TV screen. *'Go back, Austin!'*

On the screen was a long-distance silhouette of a large church in a city block. It was beautiful: a stone house of God, with a broad-shouldered spire.

Like Austin, thought Macey. The church is shaped like Austin.

From close up, the church was under siege. The neighbourhood was nothing but chain-link and rolls of razor wire; boards over windows; splintered steps and the fat slick assault of graffiti; broken bottles and—

And a body on the pavement.

It had not been covered.

It was splayed over cement, and the cement itself was broken, with weeds growing through, and the wrappings of fast food were blowing gently against the corpse. Groups of people stood staring at it. They did not seem surprised.

It was just a pile of cloth, like the homeless drunks who had been lying in the flower beds, and it was equally difficult to imagine that a person was inside the cloth. It seemed too limp, too flat, to have been alive.

The camera moved in for a close-up of blood, but there wasn't much.

'Probably some eighteen-year-old selling drugs,' said Papa. 'Austin, change the channel. We don't watch crime.'

But the story was over.

Macey could not breathe. She was pawing Austin's arm for the remote. She snatched it from him, clicked it, thrust it forward and snapped it in the air to get the picture back.

'Macey, the segment's over,' said Grace. 'You can't get it back. There's nothing wrong with the TV.'

Macey dropped the remote on the counter, but it hit the rim and fell to the floor, and she whispered, 'Give me the phone,' and Aus said, 'It's right here, Mace, here's the phone, what's the matter, what's wrong?'

'*Didn't you recognize the church?*'

'No.'

'Good Shepherd,' she said, 'it was Good Shepherd.' She got directory assistance. She named the city. She asked for the number for the Church of the Good Shepherd.

The phone was busy.

'Are you sure?' said Austin. 'Are you sure it was our Good Shepherd?'

'The door. The bulkhead door. The parking lot fence. The wire windows over our Sunday school room. The sixes. It's our church.' She punched Redial.

Grace said quietly, 'I recognized it too.'

Nana said, 'What are you talking about? That most certainly was not our church.'

Still busy.

Macey was gasping in huge scoops, like shovelfuls of sand, and the air was not working, any more than sand would, and Austin said, 'What did you see? I didn't see it. Tell me.'

'Pink sneakers,' said Macey.

He felt himself thickening, like pudding, growing heavy and sluggish.

82

His mind flashed to Venita's pink-sneakered foot on Isaiah's chest.

He heard her farewell. *Good night, sweet Prince, and flights of angels . . .*

He saw the corpse on the sidewalk.

Everything had been black and grey and white: everything except the shoes on the feet of the body.

'No, Mace,' said Austin. 'Probably lots of people with pink sneakers.'

'High-tops? Standing outside the Church of the Good Shepherd? On a school afternoon?'

Macey punched Redial again.

The line was busy.

The church phone stayed busy.

Grace called information for Reverend Warren's number, but there were nine people named Warren. Grace wrote them down and left the paper on the counter, in case somebody else – not her – wanted to do something.

Austin called four and got the right number on the fifth.

Macey took the phone out of his hand. Austin did not protest. He had no idea what to say.

'Reverend Warren? This is Macey Clare. I'm the girl whose hair got burned the day we came to help paint, and I painted with Venita. Was that Venita on the pavement? On the news? It wasn't Venita, was it?' Macey wanted a calming minister's voice, a voice of comfort and soothing quotes. But either Reverend

Warren was out of comfort or he was not that kind of minister. 'It was Venita,' he said sadly.

'*No!*' cried Macey, and she felt their hands on her: the hands of Nana and Papa and Grace and Austin, as if they wanted to take the phone away. She hunched into herself, shrugging off their hands, and stepped out of the circle, to be one with the phone.

'She stepped into the middle of a gang fight,' said Reverend Warren. He sounded desperately tired. Macey could not match this sagging voice with the big man she remembered. 'Venita knew better,' said Reverend Warren. 'But she was mad at them for shooting where there were so many little kids gathered, and she stormed out to yell at them. I guess she thought she could make them behave.'

Macey had seen Venita like that. Marching down a hall to yell at cigarette smoke.

'She finished her room, though, and she was proud of her colours. The colour of sunshine, she told me, and crowns of gold.' The minister's sigh emptied Macey's heart. 'It's a bitter business,' he told her. 'If you would like to come to the funeral, it's Thursday at two.'

Macey did not sleep.

She knew Austin hadn't slept either.

She hadn't called him.

She just knew.

They were alive, and not asleep. Venita was dead, and asleep for ever.

When morning arrived at last, the sky growing light, and the time to give up on sleep and get out of bed had come, she could hardly make herself stir. Bed seemed safe and protected. She trudged downstairs, not yet dressed for school. Dad had already galloped out to start the car. It was cold again today, no sign of spring, never mind summer, and he would warm it up a little for Mom.

Mom was elegant in black and ivory, a lime green scarf and silver earrings.

Venita filled Macey's sight like a poster on the wall, but they had talked enough about Venita last night.

'Mom, tell me more about Mr Sibley.'

'Mr Sibley?' said her mother, surprised. 'He had the best science experiments. He was a ham. His demonstrations were such fun you could hardly wait for the next day, to see what he would do then.' Mom downed a glass of orange juice, snapped her briefcase shut, checked herself in the mirror and headed after Dad.

'And he was black,' said Macey.

Her mother paused to thread her fingers through the tiny bit of hair Macey had left. Macey'd given her parents orders to stop talking about her hair, although she herself thought about it constantly. She still smelled smoke and tasted cotton.

'Black as night,' said her mother, tucking the short waves in new directions.

'Why didn't you tell me that in the first place?'

'Because it mattered then, but it doesn't matter now. Times have changed. Colour isn't first place. You have a good day in school, sweetheart. Try not to think about Venita. It's so sad, darling, but there is nothing you can do.'

They kissed goodbye, and Mom got into the car as

Dad backed out. He drove off the way he always did, like a teenager with a Corvette, because they had seconds to spare if they were to catch their train.

When the car disappeared around the corner, Macey felt a queer anguish, as if they had driven away for ever.

Was that supposed to comfort me? she thought. Mom saying not to think about it – there's nothing I can do?

She felt cold and awful, and it was a great relief when the bus finally arrived to take her to school, where she would have company and other things to think about.

The school bus felt regulated and safe, as if everything would always be neatly packaged in bright yellow, and arrive on time, and stop for signals.

Everybody on it was white.

She pictured Elizabeth Eckford, age fifteen, getting on this school bus. People would be friendly and nice and ordinary, and the fact that Elizabeth Eckford came in a black skin would not mean a single thing.

But that was not true, and she knew it was not true. People would be friendly and nice and ordinary . . . and Elizabeth Eckford, age fifteen and black, would sit alone.

Macey took a deep, shuddery breath.

Try not to think about Venita.

How could she think about anyone else? Elizabeth Eckford, four decades ago, Macey could think about for a minute; but Venita was now. Was dead. Had no now.

Was not there to paint walls yellow, quote Shakespeare, babysit the sixes or give hairstyle advice.

If only Mom had said, Think about Venita.

*

The following morning was Thursday.

'But I can't go to school today,' said Macey. 'The funeral is at two!'

'Macey,' said her mother, 'you will attend school. Your father and I are going to work, there is nobody to take you to that funeral, you would be totally out of place anyway, it would not make you feel better, it would not accomplish a thing.'

'I want to go!'

'That is absolutely out of the question, Macey!' said her father, getting very close to shouting. They were not a shouting family. 'You knew this girl two hours! You are not going into that dangerous city to her funeral.'

'I need to!'

Inside herself, Macey had been screaming for two days. Her throat ought to be sore from all that yelling, but it hadn't been out loud. Austin seemed deaf, walking without hearing, as if his thoughts about Venita had sealed him with tape; whereas her thoughts about Venita were exploding her. Grace, unbelievably, had actually asked Macey what she was upset about. Here was Venita filling Macey's thoughts as a body fills a coffin, but Grace had just said politely, 'I didn't get to know her, Mace. I'm sorry in a basic sort of way, but I'm not weeping about it. She's just a statistic for me. I know I sound heartless, but they have so many murders in that city.'

Macey was desperate for somebody else to feel the way she did. 'Grace, my mother said not to think about her,' she'd told her friend.

'That sounds like good advice.'

'Grace! You have to think about people! It

dishonours them if you don't think about them. If I were shot and killed, wouldn't you think about me?'

'I'd collapse if you were killed. But Mace, this is a stranger, and she was a stranger to you too. I think your mother's right. Don't dwell on it.'

But Macey could dwell on nothing else, and she needed to be at Good Shepherd, among people who were also dwelling on the life and death of Venita. She needed to know what they had to say; what Reverend Warren thought the Lord had to say; what Venita's grandmother was saying, and how she was enduring this terrible thing.

'You do *not* need to,' said her father. 'It is a danger-ous, dangerous place. You nearly died in a fire, and she *did* die in a fire of gunshots. You may not go.'

Macey forced herself to calm down. 'She lived there, Daddy.'

'And I'm sorry. It's a terrible world. And you're not going into it.'

'I want to go. I want to hear what Reverend Warren says. I want to meet her grandmother and her little brothers.'

'Nonsense. You'd be the only white person there.'

'It isn't nonsense! She's dead. That's not nonsense. And you said yesterday morning colour isn't first place, so – so what if I'm the only white person there?'

Venita had been burned after all. The city and the school and the poverty had burned her from birth. Gangs had finished the job.

'I have to do something!' said Macey. 'You don't understand. She meant something to me.'

'And that's fine,' said her mother with teeth-gritted

patience. Mom didn't want to miss her train. 'You've always been able to make friends easily. But there is nothing you can do.'

'There has to be!'

'Mace, honey,' said her father, 'you took a little excursion into hell, and it was good for you; it's forced you to think. But you don't bring this stuff home with you. You don't hold yourself accountable. You are not responsible because Venita was in the wrong place at the wrong time.'

'Daddy, her whole life seems to have been in the wrong place at the wrong time and mine always in the right place at the right time. It isn't fair.'

Her parents agreed that it wasn't fair.

'I have to do something,' said Macey pleadingly. 'I was there, Mom. I saw. It's my job now.'

'What job?' said her father.

'I don't know yet. I'm trying to think it through. But I owe Venita something.'

'Oh, stop it!' said her mother, who never raised her voice to Macey; never had to. 'I am sick of this nonsense. You cannot save the world, Macey. It's unfortunate that some people are born to bad situations, but there is nothing you can do. Now get dressed, have your orange juice and do not miss your bus.'

Everything she touched reminded Macey that Venita had no touch.

Venita could not put those long slim fingers on anything and feel texture, or heat, or cold.

Macey had fifteen minutes before the bus arrived at

the corner, and it was miserable out, threatening snow this late in the season, and she didn't want to stand on the corner with a bunch of people who hadn't met Venita.

She balanced her father's book about the fifties on the hall table and read standing up. There was one other chapter on segregation.

The nine students were admitted to the white high school because the federal government forced it. It turned out to be war: two thousand against nine. The black kids were kicked, tripped, hit from behind; they had hot soup poured on them in the cafeteria. Their books were stolen and their lockers smashed.

But it was the name-calling that made Macey cringe.

In seventh grade she had wanted to be best friends with Lisa. One day she spotted Lisa with her girlfriends, and hurried down the hall to catch up to them and be part of their world, and Lisa said, laughing, and pointing at Macey, 'Here comes toilet paper, wiping up the rear,' and Macey wept for days and wanted to move to California so she'd never see Lisa again. That was three years ago, and still whenever she met Lisa, she felt like crying.

She could not imagine those nine kids sticking it out, week after week, getting called ugly names again, again, again, again.

There was a nursery rhyme: sticks and stones may break my bones, but names will never hurt me. Wrong. Names hurt all the time, and they hurt a lot, and they went on hurting.

Her mind would not lie down. It leaped like a

mountain goat from crag to crag. It leaped from Venita to Elizabeth Eckford to Austin to Chamique to Lisa to Grace . . . *to Mr Sibley*.

What does he have to do with anything? thought Macey.

She knew two things about Mr Sibley. What he taught: science. And his colour: black.

Somebody had wanted him, or they would not have hired him. A lot of people must have wanted him, to get the hiring accomplished. But somebody had not wanted him, or the barn would not have been burned down around him.

I don't know that, she thought. Maybe the fire was accidental, and he just happened to live there, and it just happened that he was the first black teacher, and maybe it was a fire so ordinary you could mix it up with a beach bonfire, and maybe the fire in 1959 near my mother has nothing at all to do with a fire in 1997 that caught me.

And maybe it does.

Two o'clock.

Reverend Warren, who had welcomed them in the name of Jesus Christ, would be praying for the soul of Venita Loomis.

But Macey stood in the media centre not in church. Mrs Johnson had got the time blocks rearranged and all her classes were gathered together.

Across the room, Austin slouched against the wall with his class. 'This is your chance,' said Mrs Johnson, 'to create web pages seen by the entire world.'

'Assuming anybody in the entire world would ever visit a school page,' said Max. 'This has the potential to be a truly loser site. But I admit, I'm dying to be part of it.'

Dying.

Good night, sweet Prince, and flights of angels sing thee to thy rest.

But no fifteen-year-old ever wanted rest.

Don't think about her, darling. It's so sad, but there's nothing you can do.

Just a sentence before catching a train.

Macey wanted to be at Good Shepherd, where people wept for a girl who should still be painting the world gold.

'We'll have lots of links,' said Graff, 'but it's your responsibility to make the site exciting.'

'That's way too much responsibility,' said Max.

Behind Max, and off to the side, Austin was tapping his watch and lifting his chin towards Macey. Saying: I know what time it is; I wanted to go too.

Texas is real proud of saving you.

'I'm going to do the island beaches,' said Jennifer, slipping forwards to stand next to Max. 'They're so pretty. We can get aerial shots, and little-kid-diving-off-the-pier shots, and sailboat race shots. Blue and white, the best graphic.'

Don't you love that word indigo? *Doesn't it sound bluer than blue?*

April had remained cold, but Jennifer had dressed for summer; she looked like a wedding guest in snow white slacks, a white shirt and a sea-green silk jacket.

I'm not jealous, though, I like our paint best.

'I'd do that with you, Jen,' offered Max.

Jennifer had not dressed for summer; she had dressed for Max. 'That would be great, Max!' said Jennifer. 'Do you sail? I have a Laser and our races begin next month.'

'Sailboat races and beaches are not history,' said Mrs Johnson. 'Nor may you work together. Remember, first you write the paper. Second, you get an A. Then you qualify for a web page. Jennifer, you could do the history of how the town acquired the islands. And Max, you could research the founding of the yacht clubs. Some of New York's first Wall Street moguls were involved.'

Macey was going to start sobbing. She could feel Venita in the room with her, this completely white room with enough computers to change Venita's school, with enough money and books and classroom copies for any two schools.

She tried to compose a prayer for Venita, but she could think of only two syllables. *No.* And *God.*

'Now, Evan, your idea was transportation. That's too broad. We'll split that. How about the railroad? Early turnpikes? Coasters? Those were sailing boats that carried people and supplies before there were roads. Wendy? One of those?'

'I was thinking of comparing 1997 and 1897,' said Wendy.

'OK, but let's make it a shorter period,' said Mrs Johnson. 'Contrast what the town is now with the way it was for your grandparents.'

'My grandparents live in Ohio,' said Wendy. 'I bet Macey's the only one in the entire state who lives near her grandparents.'

You live with your grandmother? Me too.

'Macey, what a good idea. You do the grandparent comparison.'

Macey's tongue was dry and thick inside the trap of her mouth. The words came out furry. 'I'm going to do an old arson that took place in 1959. The town's first black teacher got burned out of his home.'

'Oh, no,' said Mrs Johnson, 'I'm sure that's not the case. That sort of thing never happened around here. You and I will think of something better.'

Macey retreated over the carpet, feeling her way backwards along bookcases and displays.

'I want to do churches,' said Bethany. 'White steeples against blue skies are what people think of when they think of New England.'

. . . when churchyards yawn and Hell itself breathes . . .

'We're not doing travel posters,' said Mrs Johnson. 'This is a history project.'

Austin found Macey drenched in tears, as if she had just bobbed up from underwater.

She dried her face on his T-shirt. Today it was navy, with a faded Chicago skyline.

They don't even let you say your whole speech before they bury you.

6

They hadn't let Macey skip an afternoon of school for a funeral, but only a few days later, Mom had a trip to San Francisco – worth skipping school for. It was time they did something as a family, said Mom, and since Dad could arrange to go, too, Macey and her parents boarded a plane on Sunday night.

Macey fell in love with San Francisco. It was so vertical, so white and sparkly. She wasn't used to walking with her feet angled like a ballerina. The city was full of people: all walking, all the time, just as willing to trespass as Macey; and, like Dad, reading out loud from guidebooks that said where famous people lived, or had lived once, or were reputed to have lived if you stretched the facts.

'Every hill we climb, I want to have a house there most,' said Macey.

'All the running in the world,' said her father, gasping for breath, 'didn't prepare me to climb these hills. I'm wheezing like an old geezer.'

'That's because you didn't do all the running in the world. You just talked about all the running in the world.'

They ate at wonderful restaurants, food so different from what Nana and Papa prepared that Macey wondered if her grandparents were watching the right TV chefs after all. They sailed in the bay, which might be even more beautiful than Macey's own, for it had a huge great stretch of sky and long views to distant hills speckled with joyful buildings.

After locating wooden stairs that catapulted down Telegraph Hill among houses so romantic that Macey wanted to buy each one, they hit a bookstore so Dad could read up on the San Francisco earthquake. Macey wandered around for something to read. She passed a rack of classics – Thoreau and Robert Louis Stevenson and Shakespeare. *King Lear*, *Richard III* and *Hamlet*.

Macey had written to Venita's grandmother, Mrs Loomis. It had taken hours to figure out why she was writing at all, let alone decide what to say.

In her first version, Macey wrote about Venita quoting *Hamlet* and the chilling comparison between Hamlet's world and hers. But Macey ended up writing elementary-school sentences like 'I thought we could be friends' and 'I liked painting with her'. She mailed the letter, and if anything ever felt like tossing a note in a bottle into the ocean of life, this was it.

'Find anything?' said Dad.

Macey wrenched her eyes from *Hamlet* and her mind from Venita. This trip was a strategy. Her parents did not want her thinking about Good Shepherd. 'I guess not.'

That afternoon into the sparkling city came fog, so raw her bones were cold. She hadn't brought Austin's UConn cap with her, for fear of losing it, so she bought a souvenir San Francisco cap to cover her freezing skull. Then she bought another, to give Aus. They'd have matching caps. Whether Aus would wear it, thus revealing that he and Macey had a link, she did not know.

They got home Wednesday night and she'd missed three days of school. The Clares had a huge mailbox that could hold several days' mail, so they hadn't asked Nana and Papa to pick it up. Besides, Mom and Dad hated to ask Nana and Papa for anything. Macey was the one to bring in the mail. She flipped it in piles: bills, catalogues, magazines, credit card offers. There wouldn't be personal mail, because Mom and Dad used e-mail, and nobody was out there to write to Macey.

A small square envelope with her name and address written in lovely, old-fashioned penmanship appeared in the pile.

'Hey, Mace, anything good?' said Dad, coming up behind her.

'Nope.'

'What are you hiding then? A love letter from Austin?' He grinned like a puppy, thinking he knew what she held, and she didn't correct him but went upstairs to her room to read the letter.

Dear Macey,

Venita loved your letter you wrote her. She never got mail before and she always wanted some. Yours was all the mail she ever got. Venita told me about you. She thought you would come again.

I wanted my Venita to finish school and go from here, go to a good place. But life didn't let her run anywhere.

All sun and laughing, all friends and hope, taken from her on a pavement. She's done running.

She liked your true colours. I always tell my grand-
children, you look for people's true colours. Doesn't
matter about the colour. Just the true.

So you be true, and you run for Venita. Use that life
you have.

> With love from Venita's grandmother,
> Dorothy Edna Loomis

Aus was so glad to see Macey.

He had forgotten the shortness of her hair. He had
expected to see the old ponytail bobbing. Only five
days' separation and he had already forgotten things. It
made him queasy. What had his parents forgotten
about him, and what had he forgotten about them? It
was months since they'd lived together.

Macey had bought scarves for Lindsay and Grace
and a San Francisco cap for him. Aus put on the San
Francisco cap just to be polite, because if he was going
to post any town on his head, it would be Chicago, but
then Macey put a matching cap on her fringe of hair,
and he laughed, and they tapped bills.

'How was San Francisco?' he said. He'd been there
twice, so he knew how it was. It was wonderful. It was
a great town. But Macey said, 'Venita's grandmother
answered my letter.' She held it out, so he had to set his
books on the floor in order to take it and read it.

The letter was both bleak and kind. He said lightly,
'Her first name sounds like an old person's, doesn't it?
Dorothy Edna. You can tell she's the same generation as
my grandmother Monica and your grandmother
Leandra.'

Macey gave Aus the look his mother directed so

often at Dad: the old you've-let-me-down look. 'I like the part about true colours,' he said quickly.

They had no classes together. Bells were ringing.

They had no time together either. He said, 'I'll be walking home,' and Mace nodded.

He took the cap off, because they weren't allowed in classrooms, but he held the fabric between his fingers, thinking of Macey going from one cap design to another and finally settling on this one.

He and Mace would walk to Shell Beach together, because they were both going to their grandparents'. By the time biology class was over, Aus had decided against the short cuts. He was not in the mood to squeeze between the strands of barbed wire.

By the time history was over, he was thinking of high beach grass, purple and silver sand where minerals glinted in the sun, beach boulders with sheltered spots . . .

Macey fell into the category of kid who had to bring home high marks, and so she usually paid close attention in class. She kept a mental stack of her grades, and low ones killed her.

No, they don't, she thought. She put her cap into her book bag, because hats weren't allowed in class, and drew out Mrs Loomis's letter. Every time she read it, she fell deeper inside it. Her thoughts got sticky around the edges, like marshmallows at the bonfire.

By the end of school, Macey had the letter by heart.

Or it had her.

True colours. It was one of the phrases that held her

so tightly. During lessons she hardly heard, working her way through the spectrum, Macey Clare figured out her true colours.

The colour of her family was a not-thinking colour. A go on vacation, buy souvenirs, read guidebooks colour.

If she stood in the front hall of school (marble floors and two-storey pillars, fresh flowers on a shelf between the trophy cases) and waited for Austin, he would be there. They had not agreed to do that, because they didn't have to agree. They just knew. They would walk to Shell Beach together.

It came to her like a film: a video of a boy and a girl, a beach and a flower, wind and a kiss.

But whatever Dorothy Edna Loomis expected from Macey had to begin today. If Macey waited till it was convenient, time would pass. Good intentions would dwindle. Venita would evaporate like water in the sun. Only Macey's short hair would be left to show they had been together, and then her hair would grow out, and of Venita in her life there would be no sign.

She showed the letter to Grace, who read it quickly and said, 'Oh, how nice of her to answer you.' Grace was already out the classroom door, had already forgotten it, in two strides had moved on with her life.

To Macey it seemed not just a letter, but a charge; an order.

She had a sense of huge invisible choices, with huge unknown results.

When the final bell rang, Macey did not go to meet Aus after all. She went out a side exit, walked up the hill, down two blocks, and up another hill to the town library.

The librarian was helpful without being interested. It was a safe feeling, although Macey did not know why safety was required; she was just looking at a newspaper. She didn't even know the name of the newspaper for Venita's city. The librarian pointed her to a stack.

Macey started with the Saturday of the fire at the Church of the Good Shepherd, her fire. But if there was any mention of the church fire, she did not find it. Hadn't the fireman said it was part of a string of arsons? Shouldn't there be a big article? 'Another church arson' type article? But there wasn't. Not that day, and not any day afterwards that Macey could find.

Venita's murder was covered in the second section, on the second page, the day after she was shot. The report was brief. There were no witnesses. There were no suspects. Classmates were sad. Teachers grieved for lost potential.

How could there be no witnesses and no suspects? Reverend Warren had said that Venita waded right out into a gang.

Awkwardly, Macey carried the large, flapping page to the photocopier and copied Venita's paragraphs. Then she borrowed the librarian's scissors to cut it out. Venita, her life and death, took five inches.

Macey checked newsprint for the following week, but she did not find another mention of Venita. Had the police given up so quickly? Or was it too boring for the newspaper to mention again? She thrust her hand up to run her fingers through the dark silk of her hair and was startled to find so little. Phantom hair, she thought. I wonder how long before I remember that I have no hair.

Once, somebody who admired him had commissioned that statue in the square across from Good Shepherd. A man on a horse. Like the city, the statue had once been proud and strong, but it was ruined now. Still, he had had a memorial.

Macey put the five inches of photocopy that were Venita's memorial into the envelope with Mrs Loomis's letter. Then she went back to the librarian. 'I need to look up December fourth, 1959, but this time in the local paper, please.'

The librarian led her to stacked narrow drawers of microfilm, plucked out the film for the fourth quarter of 1959, and showed her how to spool the film in the machine. It was much harder to find a paragraph on the screen than when the paper was flat on the table. But eventually she turned it up.

Twenty-seven volunteer firemen rushed to Shell Road to fight a garage fire. The garage, formerly a barn, was a total loss. One car was destroyed. Chief Raspardo said, 'Buildings as old as that barn are so dry, they're impossible to save once the fire gets started. We didn't want anybody to get hurt, so we concentrated on not letting the fire spread.'

Amount of damage has not yet been assessed by the owners.

No mention of an apartment. No mention of Mr Sibley. No mention of how the fire started.

At least nobody had been hurt. But Mr Sibley's car had burned. Or somebody's car.

Macey checked the newspaper index to find another fire, see how it compared. There'd been one a month earlier, on November 1, 1959. She scrolled to that. November 1 turned out to be an oven fire. 'Thirty-three firemen respond,' said the headline.

So . . . thirty-three men arrived to put out a fire in an oven, but twenty-seven arrived and did not put out a fire in a barn.

Well, she was not a firefighter. Maybe the oven was in a three-family home with a dozen little kids at risk. Maybe the barn, roaring hot, huge old timbers ready to collapse, posed too big a risk for the firemen to get near.

She rewound slowly, stopping to catch headlines, see if she could wrap her fingers around this elusive year, 1959. October and November were about the upcoming presidential election: Kennedy and Johnson against Nixon and Lodge. It sounded so antique. She had never heard of Lodge.

When the librarian had a minute, Macey asked, 'Are there phone books going back to 1959?'

'Better than that.' The librarian showed her something called a city directory. There was one per year for the last eighty-five years. Macey hauled the fat old orange 1959 volume off the shelf. The front half of the book was alphabetical by last name, like a regular phone book; the back half, however, truly cool, was alphabetical by street.

She looked up Shell Road. It listed every house, telling who lived there, whether they owned or rented, and their phone numbers. There were her grandparents, Putnam and Leandra Macey, same address, of course, and Austin's grandparents, Henry and Monica Fent.

There were no other names Macey recognized.

There was no listing for Mr Sibley. There was no listing of a barn apartment at all. She got 1958 off the shelf, and that year did have a barn listing: a Miss Fortunato had lived there. So . . . Mr Sibley had not lived in the barn after all? She had the whole story wrong?

She flipped to the last-name section in the 1959 volume. There he was. And now she had his full name: Wade Sibley. But his address was Schoolhouse Road instead of Shell Road. How odd.

Back to the second half of the book. She looked up Schoolhouse Road. Mr Sibley was listed under the junior high itself. So they had not listed him where he lived, but where he worked. There had to have been dozens of teachers in the junior high . . . but only Mr Sibley was listed as if he lived in the classroom.

Macey thought of Martin Luther King Jr. in the books she had checked out of the library. 'You are harried by day,' he once wrote, 'and haunted by night. Humiliated by signs reading White and Coloured. Your first name is nigger. Your middle name is boy. You are living constantly at tiptoe stance, never knowing what is next . . .'

Macey felt unsettled and quaky, like a bog after a

rain, as if slimy things were going to come up through the bottoms of her bare feet. Could Mr Sibley have been listed at the junior high because it was safer if nobody knew where he lived?

She photocopied the Shell Road page for 1959 for no reason except she could not leave the library with nothing. Next to nothing on Venita. Completely nothing on Mr Sibley.

Her head ached. She could no longer remember what brilliant plan had made her stride from school. I skipped meeting Aus for this? I thought my two fires were connected. I thought I'd find a clue; I thought I'd learn something important.

The fire smouldered in her thoughts, but this time, it was 1959's fire old and stale and hopelessly out of reach.

Voting! thought Macey, remembering Nixon and Lodge.

She went back to the librarian. 'How do I find out if somebody registered to vote in 1959?'

'Town hall. It's public record. You can see anything you want.'

Austin waited near the trophy case, knowing she would appear. He had the cap on, because that was OK in the lobby, and he searched for Macey among the hundreds of departing students.

He'd rehearsed in his mind the greeting he would give, the posture he would have, the extent to which he would let the kids hanging around see what was happening between them. He was considering taking

Macey's hand when they left the building, but had not made the final decision. He wondered what it would feel like, holding hands. He wondered what temperature her hand would be, and if his own would get cold worrying about it.

But Macey didn't show up. His hands did get cold.

It was her friend Lindsay who appeared at his side and stood too close to him. 'Hi, Austin!' she said gaily.

Lindsay and Grace exhausted him, but especially Lindsay, who was too bright-eyed for his taste, as if she were always hunting, searching, poking. For what? He didn't want to know.

'Meeting Mace?' said Lindsay, as if she knew better; as if Macey had told Lindsay where she was going, but couldn't be bothered to tell Aus.

Girls wanted girls to have boyfriends, but they also wanted to tease, find any raw nerves that might be exposed, and expose them more. Austin said, 'Have a nice afternoon, Lindsay. Gotta run.' He stepped into the last of the leaving students and jogged off the school campus. When he turned the corner, his feet wouldn't move that fast any more. He slowed to a foggy walk, his thoughts harder to organize than a term paper.

He took Macey's short cuts after all, through the golf course, through the woods, behind the old supermarket, across yards, through the swamp, over every backyard of Shell Beach. It was a lot of trespass. Nobody paid the slightest attention.

He thought of Davonn and Isaiah. If Isaiah, Austin's shape and weight, but not his colour, were to take this route, people would look up. Police would be called.

Neighbours would react as if Isaiah were ten gang members at once. Isaiah would have to prove he had a right to be there. Aus had no right to be there, but nobody cared.

Clouds scudded in, darkening the sky, and by the time he reached the end of Shell Road, Mr and Mrs Macey had put on all the lights in their kitchen. If Macey was at their house, she wasn't in the kitchen with them.

He wanted Macey to be there, and he wanted to march in the door and say, 'How come you weren't where I wanted you to be? I saved your life! You could at least read my mind and wait for me when I expect you to!'

This sounded like the sort of sentence that had damaged his parents' marriage, so Aus decided against it.

He walked out on to the curl of beach that vanished into the waves, and it was so impossibly beautiful that he decided Lucky Devil's Cake was the right recipe for anybody who lived on Shell Beach. Except he'd have been a much luckier devil if Macey Clare had cared enough to meet him after school.

The town hall was a labyrinth of teeny offices with little signs sticking out sideways into the corridors. Eventually Macey found the right clerk. 'I want to see if a particular person was registered to vote in 1959,' Macey explained.

She was amazed and proud of herself. She hated going up to people and asking for things. She couldn't bring herself to sell grapefruit for the school band even when she had the list of people who had courteously been buying it for years. Mom refused to help her sell it on the grounds that Macey had to get brave and do it herself, but Macey never did, and her parents didn't want her on record as a total loser, so they bought it. All winter long, Alec and Cordelia Clare gnawed away at boxes of grapefruit from Florida.

And here she was: a young woman walking straight into town hall, calmly requesting voting records. Way to go, Mace.

'Wish I could help,' said the clerk. 'But we clean out. A person who hasn't voted in five years gets removed from the record, and 1959 is practically forty years ago. There isn't any record.'

'In an information age, we don't keep information?'

The clerk laughed. She was a pleasant woman, hair pulled back in a ponytail. It bounced cheerfully as she talked, as if connected to her speech. 'We'd drown in paperwork if we kept everything.'

'It's not even on a computer? Or microfilm?'

'Not that I know of. Not our town, anyway.'

Macey thought. 'This person was a teacher. Would there be a record . . . I don't know . . . school records, somehow?'

'That would be in the personnel department of the board of education, but even if they would let you look in a personnel file, which they wouldn't, it wouldn't include voter status, and they don't keep anything after ten years anyway. You should have asked twenty years ago. But hey – I bet you weren't born then.'

They both smiled. 'Who are you looking for?' the woman asked.

'A man named Wade Sibley.'

'Who was he? What did he do?'

'He was my mother's seventh-grade teacher,' said Macey, and a truly brilliant lie came to her. 'I'm trying to track him down to invite him to a fiftieth-birthday party for my mom.' Why am I lying? she thought.

'That's so neat!' cried the clerk, looking around with an eager frown, ready to throw herself into the search for Wade Sibley. But there was no place to look.

Papa picked her up. 'Macey, darling, your parents will be very late in the city, catching up on work they missed from going to San Francisco, so you'll stay over with us. Did you have a good day? How was school?'

'School was fine. Papa, rack your brains. Remember something about Mr Sibley and the barn fire for me.'

'Are you still bogged down in 1959?' said Papa, laughing. 'It's your hair. Tell you what, we'll get you a wig. Want to be a frosted bouffant blonde?'

Last night she'd asked Mom about 1959, and Mom had replied that she'd got her first Barbie that year.

If they thought talking about teased hair and Barbie dolls would make her forget Mr Sibley and 1959, they had a crummy strategy. The more they slid away from her questions, the more she noticed.

Mrs Loomis's letter entered Macey's soul again, and the taste of her cinnamon-icing sticky buns suddenly came into Macey's mouth – a food memory to go along with her smoke memory.

At the intersection, they had to wait for about twenty cars to turn in front of them.

Every driver and every passenger was white.

The only colours the town came in were white and pink.

It was true in school.

It was true on Shell Road.

It was true in church.

It was true in the town hall.

It was true. This was a pink-and-white town. And in 1959, it was not only pink and white, if it took burning down barns to do it, the town meant to stay that way.

And it had.

She looked at her grandfather and thought, Which neighbour did start that fire?

She killed the thought. It was too sick, too horrible. But she was tasting smoke again, and she said, 'Papa, who were Mom's other teachers? They'd have known. Mr Sibley. Are any of them still around?'

'I wouldn't have known even in 1959,' said Papa. 'Back then the wives handled school while the men earned the living. Ask your grandmother. Actually, don't ask your grandmother; she gets snappish when you bring up that silly fire. Ah, here we are. And we're having plain old lemon chicken with saffron rice.'

I have to find a person who would have known Mr Sibley, she thought. Who would he have hung out with? What did people do in groups? In 1959? Did they . . . go bowling? Coach Little League? Go to church?

Church! She glanced at the car clock. Six minutes before five. The church office closed at five.

Papa pulled into his driveway and Macey yanked open the car door, dashed inside and grabbed the telephone. 'Hi, it's Macey Clare. I was just wondering, do you happen to know who was church secretary in 1959?'

Her grandfather came in behind her. She looked up at him. It was not her sweet chef in the kitchen Papa who looked back. It was the attorney he had once been, cold and hard. Macey dropped her eyes to the phone.

The current secretary muttered to herself for a while. 'Hmmm. Well, there have been very few church secretaries. It seems to be the kind of thing people stay with. I think it must have been Stella Miller.'

'Is she still around?'

'Sure is. She's in the nursing home up in the north part of town. She's got to be a hundred. Ninety, any way. The minister visits every Thursday afternoon to say hi.'

'Does she say hi back? Is she still with it?'

'Yes and no. She'd probably remember everything from 1959, but nothing much about this year.'

Perfect, thought Macey. 'Am I allowed to visit her or do I need, like, a permission slip or something?'

'They will be absolutely thrilled that a person under sixty-five is visiting.'

Macey hung up.

Papa and Nana did not know they had got somewhat deaf. Their voices from the kitchen were loud and clear.

Papa: '. . . obsessing on that fire.'

Nana: ' . . . the less said, the better.'

*

Macey called him that night. Austin had just put her cap on a hook and was staring at it from the other side of his bedroom. 'Aus,' she said to him, 'will you do something with me?'

He felt jumbled and unsteady. 'Anything.'

'Now that you have a driver's licence, would you drive me someplace?'

'Yes.' He felt as if his answer should be longer. But yes covered all he had to say.

'This may not be on your list, Aus. I want you to drive me to a nursing home to interview an old lady there.'

'You're right. Not on my list.'

'I'm serious,' she said anxiously, as if he would refuse now, and she would be stranded.

'OK, I'm putting it on my list. I'll borrow the car from Grandfather. Maybe it can count for community service credit.'

'You have enough credits, and this is private, OK?'

'OK.'

'Saturday afternoon?' she said.

'Saturday afternoon,' he promised.

Saturday morning, before Aus picked her up for the nursing home trip, Macey was sitting at the breakfast table with Mom and her girlfriend Mrs Framm and a pot of coffee.

'You know who is still around?' said Mrs Framm. 'Bonnie.'

'Bonnie!' exclaimed Macey's mother. 'I haven't thought of her in a hundred years.'

Macey loved the gossip of grown-ups, especially about old school acquaintances. Her own brilliant, sophisticated mother could still get furious over a slight from fifth grade. It made Macey feel so much better about holding a grudge against Lisa. Mom and Ginger Framm loved to discuss who had not succeeded who ought to have; who'd got fat and disgusting who had certainly looked better thin; and best of all, who turned out to be boring who had called herself creative.

But Mrs Framm turned to Macey with this particular gossip. 'Bonnie,' Mrs Framm explained to Macey, 'would remember Mr Sibley very well. She became a science teacher because of him. Mr Sibley changed Bonnie's life. She became a Freedom Rider in the sixties because of Mr Sibley. He was the first black person she ever met and the best teacher she ever had and she decided to teach high-school chemistry in his honour.'

'That's so sweet,' said Mom.

It isn't sweet, thought Macey. It's profound. It's important. But it isn't sweet.

Ginger Framm was a committee woman who never omitted a detail and certainly never postponed till tomorrow what might be done this minute. She whisked up the kitchen phone, called Bonnie, and said in an organizing voice, 'Bonnie. Cordelia Macey Clare's daughter is doing a school paper on Mr Sibley, remember, that seventh-grade science teacher you had and I didn't? Talk to her about him, OK? She has lots of questions.'

Macey took the phone nervously. 'This is so nice of you, Bonnie,' she said lamely. She didn't like calling

113

grown-ups by their first names. It felt as if she'd arrived at a party wearing the wrong clothes.

'There's nobody I'd rather talk about than Mr Sibley!' said Bonnie, who had surely been a cheerleader. 'I'm so thrilled that somebody is going to do him justice.'

What did that mean? Do him justice? Macey felt strangely afraid.

'He was such a fine man,' said Bonnie. 'What teaching technique!'

Macey pulled herself together. 'Actually, I'm mainly interested in the fire.'

'What fire?' said Bonnie.

'The fire in December where he lost his home.'

Bonnie was puzzled. 'I don't remember anything like that. Are you sure it was Mr Sibley?' She launched into excited descriptions of chemistry experiments, and gravity experiments, and electricity experiments.

Macey could not get a grip on this ancient story. How come people didn't remember this fire? 'How long was he at the junior high?' she asked.

'Just the one year. We were so incredibly lucky to have had him.'

'How old was he?'

'Twenty-two. He had just graduated from college. He changed lives. Every kid who had Mr Sibley went on to work for civil rights in the sixties and seventies.'

Macey was impressed. 'Every kid?'

'Well, that's probably an exaggeration. In fact, that's ridiculous. I have no idea. I've kept up with maybe a dozen people from school. And I guess not all of them cared about civil rights. I guess, if I'm truthful, four of us.' Bonnie laughed a little less happily. 'Yes. Four of us that I know of. But still, that's a lot, when you think of the world. He made four of us better people.'

Macey was so glad she had Aus along.

There was something scary and wrong about a nursing home; a place to stack old, infirm, unwanted people. When they turned down the hallway that would take them to Stella Miller's room, Macey could taste the nursing home. A mixture of Clorox and old age and medicine and cooking. Old, tired cooking, cabbage or onions, hour after hour, till it hung in the air and you tasted it when you breathed. Poor, poor Stella Miller. Poor everybody in this building.

How old would Mr Sibley be? Twenty-two in 1959 and now it was 1997, so he would be sixty. Good. If she found him, he would not be in a nursing home.

Macey had expected that a woman a hundred years old would be thin and wispy and frail and pale, but Stella Miller was immense and tanned and demanding that somebody be her bridge partner.

'I don't play bridge,' said Macey.

'Learn,' said Stella Miller. 'It's a very important skill in adult life. Without a good game of cards, this is a difficult world.'

'Could I ask about 1959? Was that a difficult world?'

'Nineteen fifty-nine,' said Stella Miller. 'Give me a hint. What was happening in 1959?'

'A family named Macey lived on Shell Road, and a family named Fent. Do you remember any of them?'

'Remember them all. Fine people.'

'And a stable burned down with the science teacher in it,' said Macey. 'Do you remember that? I'm researching the fire.'

'Oh, good heavens. Of course I remember the fire. The important thing wasn't that he taught science. The important thing was that he was the first coloured teacher we had in this town. Naturally everybody hated him.'

Macey's hair prickled. 'I'm sure they didn't hate him,' she said quickly. 'They were just uncomfortable.'

'Well, you don't burn a building down around somebody because you're uncomfortable. It's hate, that's what it is. They hated him.'

Macey looked away from Stella Miller and towards Aus, but he was staring out the window to let her know this was her interview, not his. She said, 'Who hated him most?'

'Oh, the parents. They didn't want their children to answer to a Negro. Back then you said Negro. If you were polite. People in this town are always polite. You've got to imagine a world where coloured people weren't worth much but teachers were worth a lot. Weren't paid a lot, but they got respect. It's the other way around now. But back in the nineteen fifties, you expected your child to obey the teacher. Respect the teacher. Grow up to be like the teacher. And now the teacher is a Negro? Nope. Can't have it. So you take the child out of the school – or you get the Negro to leave. Simple.'

So Ginger's parents had chosen the first way. Taking the child out of school.

116

And what way had Cordelia Clare's parents chosen?

Macey held herself very still. 'Mr Sibley taught only one year,' she said to Stella Miller. 'Did he leave because of the fire?'

'Sure. Who wants to live someplace where you really and truly aren't wanted?'

Maybe Mr Sibley had not known he really and truly wasn't wanted. What a way to find out. 'Do you remember anything about the fire?'

'No. But you could ask the fire chief. In 1959 that would have been Vinnie Raspardo. He's still alive.'

Macey'd read that in the newspaper and forgotten it. 'Who do you think started the fire?' she said.

Stella Miller shifted her great weight and stared at Macey. 'What did you say your name is?'

Stella Miller remembered her grandparents well, remembered the Fents well too. So Macey changed her name. It shocked her to hear a fake name come out of her mouth. 'Marcy Smith.' She did not look at Austin. She could not imagine what he thought of her now. She could not think of an explanation for this lie. She had lied to the clerk in the voting office too.

'And what is this project for?' said Stella Miller.

'Black History Month,' said Macey, although that was February and this was April. 'You know, the town's first black teacher.'

Stella Miller said, 'OK, so you don't play bridge. What can you play? Gin rummy? Canasta?'

'I can play double solitaire,' said Austin.

He and Stella Miller played double solitaire. Stella Miller won. Dealing out cards for another game with incredible swiftness, she said, 'Who started the fire? It's an interesting question. They never investigated, as far as I know.'

Never investigated? That was impossible. Of course they investigated.

Stella lined up the cards. Most were hidden.

'Think about it,' she said. 'Who was threatened the most? Those people on Shell Road. With all their money and their fine cars and their trips to Europe and their private beaches – think they wanted a Negro living next door?'

No, thought Macey Clare. Not these answers. I don't want these answers.

7

'Austin,' said his grandfather. His voice was serious.

Austin stiffened. Grandfather was going to talk about Chicago or divorce or parents. Austin wasn't ready. He kept moving the tack cloth over the hull of the little boat they were restoring, picking up invisible dust from sanding. Then he smiled at his grandfather. Whatever phone call Grandfather had had from Mom or Dad, whatever news he possessed that Austin didn't, Austin would take calmly.

But there was no calm in him. He felt as weak as if his legs had been torn off and he had nothing to stand on. Don't let them divorce, he thought. Don't let them.

'I have a sense that you're becoming friends with Macey Clare,' said his grandfather.

Austin folded the tack cloth and set it down. They weren't going to talk about Chicago or divorce or parents. They were going to talk about girls. Probably Grandfather had lots of knowledge, but none Austin wanted to hear out loud. He picked up the can of varnish and reread the instructions.

Macey.

Over Macey he was spinning like a comet. Trajectory unknown.

On the beach, surrounded by stars and ocean, he

119

had felt himself just as elemental: a tide of desire. When she called the other night, his heart might have been answering the phone. And then, instead of an ordinary suburban date of movie, popcorn and back row, they'd gone on that visit to Stella Miller.

He felt sick from it. He could not get the taste out of his mouth. He felt as if Macey were driving a new car towards a high cliff. He didn't want to be in that car with her, but he didn't want to be anywhere else either.

'Perhaps, Austin, you could talk to Macey about this project she seems to have taken on,' said his grandfather.

Austin blinked. 'OK.'

'She's talking to everybody about the fire that destroyed the old barn apartment,' said Grandfather. 'It's a sad story, Austin, and one we would all prefer not to have dredged up. I think you could help her find another outlet for her energy.'

Austin was astonished. His grandfather wanted him to corner Macey and tell her to stop researching the fire?

Those people on Shell Road. With all their money and their fine cars and their trips to Europe and their private beaches – think they wanted a Negro living next door?

'What is the story, Grandfather?' he said carefully. He tried to think about this without thinking too much. 'What's sad about it? Is she right? Did the guy die in the fire?'

'Austin, if I were comfortable with the story, I wouldn't mind Macey stirring the ashes,' said Grandfather. 'I do not want to discuss it myself, and I do not want other people discussing it.'

Austin imagined a drink mixer, a slender crystal rod, thrust into yesterday's cold and sodden fire. You didn't stir the ashes because a spark might have stayed hot, and when oxygen reached the spark, a second fire would kindle. 'Macey is just kind of cruising past it, I think, Grandfather. I mean, she did lose her hair in a fire, so fire kind of billowed up in importance, and once she gets the answers she wants, she'll leave it behind.'

The sloping wrinkles of Grandfather's face hardened. His eyelids lowered until the glint of his pupils was barely visible. The combination of old puckered skin and slit eyes was reptilian. Austin had to look away. 'Why don't you just talk with Mace, Grandfather?' he said uneasily. 'Let her know what the story is, and answer her questions, and—'

'I made it clear,' said Grandfather, 'that I would like you to redirect Macey. Unless things have changed greatly since I was sixteen, you are in a position to do that.'

Things *had* changed greatly since Grandfather was sixteen. Ordering Macey around would be a really poor choice.

On the other hand, this was his grandfather, who was giving him a home and asking nothing in return. Except this.

'OK,' said Austin, and he wondered if the word *OK* was a promise, or if it was just the word *OK*.

Macey's parents usually got home on the 7:08 train and then drove to the house, so they got back around 7:20 every night. After he got home, her father in particular seemed to need a half hour in which to do nothing. He'd unlace his shoes and pad aimlessly around. Mom liked to poke – open the mail, make lists, inventory the refrigerator. There was nothing in the refrigerator tonight, so somebody was going to have to think of a food solution. Mom took boxes out of the cupboard – pasta, rice, instant mashed potatoes – and examined them for clues.

Macey was reeling with her own new clues.

Somebody had meant Venita to die. Somebody had chosen her, aimed at her and ended her.

And Mr Sibley? Had Mr Sibley been meant to die?

You don't burn a building down around somebody because you're uncomfortable. It's hate, that's all it is. They hated him.

The mobs she had read about in Alabama and Arkansas and Mississippi had been horrible but honest. They went right out there in the street and called names. They faced the network cameras while they shouted their threats.

Think about it. Who was threatened the most?

It's all about threats, thought Macey. Venita and Isaiah, Davonn and Chamique; they are a threat to us. They are a threat to this town. Black is a threat. My parents wouldn't even let me go to a church and a funeral, it's that much of a threat.

And who, in 1959, was threatened by Mr Sibley? And therefore became a threat to Mr Sibley? *Those people on Shell Beach.*

We didn't call names, did we? thought Macey Clare. We cut right to the chase. We used a match.

Her body seemed to change its chemistry: it was no longer blood and bone. It was something fierce and needful. She would never know who started the fire at Good Shepherd, but she had to know who had started the fire on Shell Beach. Who burned the barn? Who planned for Wade Sibley to die?

Was it my very own grandfather?

'Mom?' she said politely. 'Why didn't you bring Mr Sibley a plate of cookies?' Her mother stared uncomprehendingly over a box of macaroni. 'You said when a new teacher moved into the barn, you always brought a casserole or dessert to welcome them. But you never went into Mr Sibley's apartment. You said, *of course* you never did.'

Mom set the box on the counter and tilted it to read the recipe on the back for penne rigate with mascarpone cheese. The odds that this particular kitchen would have mascarpone cheese hanging around were about a zillion to one. 'Well, my parents were a little uncomfortable with the whole thing.'

'What whole thing?'

'Macey, don't be dense. People weren't that sure of themselves when integration began. Now, let's have a real dinner for a change, so you can report to Nana and Papa that I still know how to use a stove. I found an onion and some frozen chopped peppers to throw into the macaroni.'

'I don't think you *do* still know how to use a stove,' said Dad. 'I know *I* don't. It must be Macey who knows how to use a stove.'

'You cook, Mace,' agreed Mom. 'All that time you spend in your grandparents' kitchen should have paid off by now.'

For a minute Macey hardly knew who these well-dressed, attractive people were. Why won't they talk? she thought. Why won't anybody talk? Because nobody ever wants to talk about race?

She put some oil in a pan and browned the onion and peppers. That's why I'm lying when I ask questions, she thought. I don't want to talk about race, either. I don't even want to admit that that's my topic. And if I do have to admit that's the topic, I want to pretend I was forced into it. It's an assignment. Or a party plan.

But what if it isn't race they're staying away from?

What if they won't talk because they know who started the fire?

Macey wanted to pin her mother to the wall and force her to answer, but her mother was far too strong for Macey. Next to Cordelia Clare, Macey felt like a pale copy, a Xerox, whereas Mom was the real thing.

She could not place demands on her mother; in this family, it worked exclusively in the other direction.

It had been more than two weeks since Venita's murder; four weeks since Saturday Group went to paint. Macey could no longer quite picture the girl she had known only two hours. She could not remember the exact shade of yellow in the paint can. She had lost the quotes from *Hamlet*.

But the words of Dorothy Edna Loomis she had by heart.

After dinner, Macey pulled out the 1959 city directory page for Shell Road. Then she got the current phone book and looked up every single name. Of the forty-two names listed in 1959, three still lived on Shell

Road in the same houses (including the Fents and the Maceys); one lived on Shell Road, but in a different house; three lived in town, but not on Shell. She started calling.

With the first people, she said she was Macey Clare, doing a school research project on a fire that had occurred on Shell Road in 1959, and did they remember the burning of a barn?

No.

Did they remember a Mr Sibley, the first black teacher in the town?

No.

Did they have any suggestions for who might remember?

Aren't you related to the Maceys who live on Shell Road? they said. Your grandparents could tell you what you need to know.

'Well, I have to use lots of sources,' she said lamely. 'You know, school papers and all.'

They wished her good luck, and Macey hung up, so embarrassed she had to leave the room so the telephone didn't laugh at her.

It was one thing to use a phone to order pizza, or find out what movie was playing, or call Grace to gossip. But phone research was like asking for a date, which she had never done, though she often rehearsed. Every night she decided to call Aus and then decided not to call Aus and then decided yes, she would call Aus after all. When she woke up, it was morning, and no phone call had taken place. What she actually wanted to do was quit high school and move in with him, and yet the only time she picked up the phone was to demand a ride to a nursing home.

She dialled the second name, a family still in town but no longer on Shell Road. The man's 'Hello?' was already grumpy. He probably expected a telemarketer begging him to change phone companies. Quickly she filled the silence.

'Hi, I'm Marcy Smith, I'm a sophomore in high school, and I've been assigned to write up the first black teacher in town for a Black History Month Project. Do you by any chance remember a Mr Sibley who briefly had an apartment on Shell Road when you lived there?'

'Yes,' the man said.

'You do?'

He called his wife to the phone.

So she was on the phone with Mike and June, and they were saying, 'Well, Marcy, it wasn't a pretty thing. Doubt if folks are proud of how they behaved. Why, the banker that lived down there wouldn't let the black guy open an account. 'Course, that had to be stopped right away, wasn't legal, didn't want people to think we were Southerners or something. So people spoke harsh to him, and he let the black guy have a bank account after all. But they were really fussed about it, that couple. They said it would ruin property values and wasn't good for the children.'

Macey was writing it all down. She had started a notebook after talking to Stella Miller, so she could check later to see exactly what had been said. 'What else did people do about the black teacher?'

'Talked a lot. There were church meetings, to get

126

people to talk about their feelings and be Christian. That was back before you talked about feelings, remember. In the fifties, you weren't supposed to have feelings, let alone talk about them.'

'Although you *were* supposed to be Christian,' said June dryly, on her extension.

'I was up in the apartment once,' said Mike, 'because I'm a plumber, and I redid the plumbing. Sweet little place. Cute little cabinets with little green apple handles. Wonderful view. Would have liked to live there myself.'

'Every autumn,' said June, 'it was a struggle finding housing for teachers. You'd have all these new teachers, because back then, if a woman had a baby, she stopped working, so there was more turnover than there is now. And here the best apartment is going to a coloured man.'

'Did you ever meet him?' said Macey.

'Just the night of the fire. Everybody met him then.'

'Would you tell me about the fire?'

'I ran down there, of course,' said Mike, 'to see if I could help, and the guy was standing alone in the road, kind of froze up, and I remember not knowing what to say to him. Place burned to the ground. They didn't save nothing. And his car, it was an old VW Beetle, you don't hardly see those around now, and the fire marshal said the fire was intentional, he knew because of the way the car burned. An accelerant had been poured all over the car. I remember because I had never come across arson before.'

An accelerant had been poured over the car.

So Mr Sibley had been upstairs in his own home, while downstairs some person slipped inside with a can of gasoline or kerosene and sloshed fuel on the very car that took Mr Sibley back and forth to school, and then lit a match.

It's hate, that's what it is.

Oh, yes, it was hate.

Nothing else could make you do such a thing, especially knowing that the torch of the car would become the torch for the barn, and upstairs – standing on an old wooden floor, a floor that could not be saved, a floor the firemen would not even try to save – was the man who would be trapped by that fire.

And you were glad; you hated him; he was coloured.

'What happened to the teacher?' said Macey. She was shaking. She could hardly hold the telephone. An emotion that was neither hate nor fear, but something equally strong, something she could not identify, because she had never felt it before, had sloshed over her, as if she too were waiting to be lit by a match.

'Where did the teacher go?'

June said, 'Let me think on this, because I used to know. I remember the house.'

'Did I do their plumbing?' said Mike.

'Yes, you did, dear. It was that house . . . oh, you know, somebody else owns it now, that red one on the side of the hill, the one that looks down on the baseball diamond.'

'Oh, right! That was – Beedon,' said Mike.

'Yes,' June told her, 'a family named Beedon took the teacher to live with them.'

Macey flipped through the phone book as they talked, but there was no Beedon listed. She tried spelling it Beadon and Biedon. Nobody was listed.

'Swordfish,' Mr Macey told Austin when he walked in from the back porch. Mr Macey always outlined the menu for a guest. 'You're a lucky man that your grandparents chose tonight for committee meetings.'

Macey had drained the potatoes. She waved at Austin and then dumped in butter and milk heated in the microwave while Nana cut in chunks of cream cheese to make it extra perfect. Macey beat it a few times with the hand masher and then whipped it with the mixer. She was as intent over the mashed potatoes as if she were taking finals.

Her cap of hair had softer edges now, and her eyes were like stars beneath her hair's dark circle.

Then Austin remembered important things. 'I'm starving,' he said. 'Let's pick up the pace.'

'Just for that,' said Nana, 'I shall waste valuable time cutting lemon slices with serrated tops like castle turrets, twisting them delicately to lie on top of the swordfish, and arranging long thin green beans as neatly as books on a shelf.' Which she did.

Finally she set the plates down, and at last they could eat. Austin had to pace himself, or he would have gulped down his entire dinner before the rest of them had balanced their forks for the first bite.

It was the kind of dinner where you didn't talk much. Sometimes Austin thought the better the food was, the less talk you needed. You could just be glad you were alive and somebody else had done the cooking.

This made him think of his parents, and a stab passed through him and then went away.

Dessert was plum-apple cake with crust on the bottom and fruit in the middle and sweet slivers of dough and sugar on top.

'Macey,' said Austin, 'let's try to see the comet tonight.'

'Hale-Bopp,' said Macey. 'I love that name. The Bopp part sounds like Hale hit his little brother over the head with a baseball bat.'

Austin had already had three helpings of cake, but he could have eaten a fourth. Nobody offered a fourth. 'You come too,' he told Macey's grandparents. 'It should be a real clear night.' He could not believe he had suggested this.

But luckily they were unwilling to walk that far, and said they would have coffee instead. Nana winked at Austin and wrapped up the rest of the plum cake for him. Papa hung on to Moose, who whined desperately to go on the walk. It was not a black Lab Aus wanted to hang on to. Papa winked at Aus too.

Austin and Macey put on jackets and walked in the dark to the beach. The wet sand was hard underfoot, not soggy. Just when you felt secure, it shifted under your shoes, throwing off your stride.

The night curled around them.

The ocean was magnificent, waves singing in the dark, star patterns tossed in the mirror of the water. It smelled different, sounded different, from Lake Michigan. Aus braced against an unexpected wave of

130

home-sickness. His thoughts spun off towards Chicago and Lake Michigan, comets and stars, and what he wanted to do with his life. He stooped and picked up pebbles, to give himself something to mess with.

'Don't you think the ocean is creepy at night?' said Macey. 'All those little sparkles on black water. Like tiny aliens advancing on the tide.'

Austin would never have characterized it like that. He smiled. 'I guess I won't be taking you to a horror movie anytime soon.'

Her eyes were two moons shining on him. He stepped towards her, but she stepped away, and he felt panicked and unwanted. His hand tightened around the pebbles and he could feel their edges, as sharp as if they had never been in the sea.

He had held her so easily in the van when he didn't even own a shirt any more and she reeked of smoke. He'd wrapped his arms around her, comforted her with the warmth of his hands, rested his face against her head. But tonight was not rescue. It was not comfort. He didn't know what it was. The strength that had enabled him to hold her against the wall while he roughed out the flames was present now, when he didn't want it, when Macey certainly would not want it. He felt like a monster truck when the situation called for a Jaguar and leather seats.

'Oh, Aus,' she said, almost in tears, and he was horrified that he had brought on tears, 'I would have said I could ignite the sand, the way I feel about you, and I can't even touch you.'

He put one hand on her short silky hair and the

131

other against her cold silky cheek, and then it was OK between them. When she tucked herself against him, he felt like sea meeting shore.

And then somehow it seemed time to speak, and he could think of nothing affectionate and just right, so like a jerk, he blurted out the sentence his grandfather had dictated.

Macey could not believe what Austin had just said to her.

His grandfather had asked Aus to stop her from talking about the barn fire? Stop her from what? What was out there?

The wind brushed salty mist across her face.

She turned her back on Aus. High above was the searing path of the comet. Nobody knew exactly what was out there. But somebody, somewhere, knew all about the fire.

The lancing emotion that had struck when she was on the phone with Mike and June almost lifted her off the sand.

'Remember how Nana talked about cooking, Aus? All the lovely waiting, she said. But it isn't lovely to wait for your fair share. And that's what they had to do, the Negro children in Little Rock, they had to stand and wait. See if anybody would let them near a fair share. And here on Shell Road in 1959, Mr Sibley got his fair share, but they wouldn't let him keep it. They burned him out of it and waited for him to run.'

Her voice whispered softer than the waves.

'Mr Sibley went to school one day and made science so real and exciting that one girl became a chemistry teacher in his honour, and the next day somebody tried to kill him. Because that's what this is, Aus. Fire is not a conversation. It's not a way to ask somebody to leave. It's a way to kill.'

Austin sat on the high stone with the blood-sacrifice pool while clouds drifted below the stars, the tide slid slowly out to sea and Macey talked. She talked about Mike and June, about Stella Miller, about newspaper reports, the books she was reading, the city directory. She talked about her parents: how every conversation had to be light and easy, like cake without calories; how angry she was that they would not ever actually answer a question.

Austin felt as if he were listening to her soul. Macey shimmered in front of him, and only when they spilled over did he realize the shimmer was tears in her eyes. And yet she did not stand like a weeper; she stood like a fighter, like a sheriff in a Western ready for the shoot-out.

'I don't believe things are meant, Aus. That's too horrible. God or the angels dictating arsons and victims and little children without toilets and a nine-year-old stabbed. I refuse to believe things are meant. But it is your responsibility to learn something. *So what about Venita?*'

He did not know where her thoughts were going. Venita had got out of the fire unscathed. There was no possible connection between Venita and Mr Sibley. Aus felt almost ambushed by Macey's emotions; he was not anywhere near her level; it was exactly like his own father with his own mother.

133

'Aus?' said Macey. 'When Nana gave you a glass of cake? Remember that?'

'Lucky Devil's Cake. As in you lucky devil, you, this is the world's best cake.'

'Yes,' said Macey. 'Yes. Stop right there. That's my question. How come we're the lucky devils, Aus? How come we have the world's best cake?'

Austin thought: This is what passion is, caring that much. This is why Mom is so mad at Dad. She says he doesn't have enough emotion. She wants this much from him.

He wanted to give Macey everything he had, every emotion and every fibre, but she took another step back on the sand. She was entirely dark against the faintly gleaming ocean. He patted the stone beside him, aching to be back where they had been half an hour ago. 'Do you feel as if Venita's fire and the barn fire are connected, Mace? I can't see it.'

She drifted towards him, slow as tides, and finally sat next to him. Their canvas jackets rasped like tent flaps.

'I know now there's not an actual mystery-type connection,' she said. She let him rest his arm around her and he did not consider anything more. The evening belonged to fire and death now. 'The two fires didn't start from the same match. But I can't let go, Aus. There *is* a connection, and I haven't got it clear, but it *will* get clear, the more I think about it. The more I ask.'

A sad story, Grandfather had said. Not to be dredged up. A dredge was a shovel for the ocean floor. It scooped up the ruined and rotted and hidden things that lay in the dark on the bottom. The ruined and rotted were still there, or Grandfather would not want Macey silenced.

'The trouble is, I ask and nobody answers. Because you know what, Aus? My true colours, our family colours,' she said softly, 'are that we don't think about anything that matters. That's our rule.'

The family colours.

The family rule.

Pain stabbed Austin's chest so severely, he wondered if a sixteen-year-old in terrific condition could have a heart attack. He could actually feel his heart go into spasm and then relax, while his chest locked and his lungs failed. He folded over himself for a moment, splinting the pain. Closing his eyes had the odd effect of making Macey's words louder and brighter.

The words of June and Mike, actually, which Macey had just quoted.

Why, the banker that lived down there wouldn't let the black guy open an account. 'Course, that had to be stopped right way, wasn't legal, didn't want people to think we were Southerners or something. So people spoke harsh to him, and he let the black guy have a bank account after all. But they were really fussed about it, that couple. They said it would ruin property values and wasn't good for the children.

Property values, thought Austin.

This is the property.

Children, thought Austin.

That would be my mother.

Banker, thought Austin.

That would be Grandfather.

Austin had cold hands, and cold dread and cold

knowledge. For now he knew the connection between Venita and Mr Sibley. It was not fire.

Both times, it was one gang teaching a lesson in territory to a trespasser.

Venita believed the street was her territory; she was a lioness stalking out to protect her cubs. But the territory belonged to people with guns, and they were stronger, and they proved it.

Mr Sibley believed he could stake out territory in a foreign land, a land that had never accepted one of his kind. But he had been wrong.

Mace had got halfway to the answer: it *was* all about dividing the cake. Who got the most icing and the biggest slice?

The beauty of Shell Beach was entirely cold now: frozen like crystal. 'Let's go inside,' he said, knowing that he had just joined the team of her parents and grandparents; he was not going to give her answers either.

At the Fent house, lights were blurry behind pulled curtains.

Back home in Chicago, Austin had not played board games since he was six and tired of Candyland. His grandparents still loved them, however, and were delighted to have a third player. Austin didn't exactly mind Parcheesi and Monopoly; it just wouldn't have occurred to him to do that for fun. Often, after dinner, he and his grandparents played Cluedo. There would be a plate of Macey's grandparents' soft molasses cookies, which folded like pancakes over Austin's fingers, turned back into dough against his tongue, and then melted down his throat. Just last night, the possible murderers in Cluedo had been strewn across the board, with their possible weapons in their possible rooms. 'Your move, Aus,' his grandfather had said cheerfully.

My move, thought Aus now, thinking of bankers and fire.

And was it my grandfather with the gas can in the barn?

Or was it Macey's grandfather with the match in the car?

8

Mom's classmate Bonnie, who had become a chemistry teacher in honour of Mr Sibley, telephoned Macey. 'I called my parents,' she said. 'They retired to San Antonio. They love it there.'

'How nice,' said Macey, casting around for something to say about San Antonio.

'I remember Mr Sibley so well,' explained Bonnie, 'and I didn't remember a fire, so I asked my parents. It was arson, they said, to drive him away.'

Bonnie's parents remembered. And Bonnie cared enough to telephone them and ask. So why didn't Macey's mother remember? Or care enough to ask?

'But it didn't work,' said Bonnie. 'Mr Sibley stayed the entire school year. He never batted an eye.'

Stella Miller had made Mr Sibley sound whipped, but Bonnie's parents made him sound like a man of courage. 'Why didn't you remember?' said Macey. 'Wasn't there publicity and rumour and gossip?'

'My parents said Mr Sibley never discussed it. Can you imagine the self-control? Think of all he lost. Car, dishes, blankets, neckties, papers. Stuff he could never replace – photos and collections. But he never mentioned the fire to his classes. He went on being a teacher and did not let it interfere.'

'That's incredible,' said Macey. 'How come he wasn't sobbing, or had bandages on his arms or borrowed shoes on his feet? How could he not have said to his kids, "This awful thing happened to me"?'

'Yeah,' agreed Bonnie. 'If that happened to me or one of my students, my classes wouldn't even let me mention chemistry. We'd talk about our pain. My parents said that back in the fifties you didn't talk about ugly things, and this was ugly, so no grown-up discussed it. Not with their kids and not with each other; and it wasn't in the newspaper either, because the purpose of the paper was to make the town look good, so it wasn't the kind of story they wrote.'

'So it wasn't really a secret,' said Macey slowly, 'but it became a secret, from not talking about it.' She imagined the secret gathering around the burning barn, spreading down Shell Road, sifting into houses, and crossing generations. 'You'd think Mr Sibley would want the kids on his side. Finding out who did it and stuff.'

'It wasn't like that in the fifties. He would not have thought of the kids as being on his side. He would have stayed the teacher, the grown-up, because anything else was weakness.' Bonnie's voice dropped to a whisper, as if still on the edge of the secret, still skirting around the truth. 'Besides, Macey, he may have known who did it. It's possible that a lot of people knew who did it. Remember, if the fire department was there, and if the police were there, and if the neighbours were there, and nobody did anything . . . then Mr Sibley would know that nobody was *going* to do anything either.'

*

Mrs Johnson had not actually accepted the 1959 arson as Macey's local history project. Come talk to me, she'd said, we'll think of a better one; but Macey had not followed up.

In an entire stack of library books, Macey found nobody who wrote about 1959, but the nineteen sixties were so full of racial struggle Macey could hardly keep track of all the cities with protests and schools with riots and groups with capital letters – NAACP, SNCC, SCLC.

June 12, 1963.

Mississippi.

Medgar Evers was a high-profile black leader who had a wife and three little kids. He was so hated by the white authorities that he actually had his kids practise hiding in the big porcelain bathtub in case the house was attacked. But he himself didn't hide. He was shot in his own driveway. One fingerprint was found on the gun that killed him: Byron De La Beckwith's, a member of the white Citizens' Council. He was never convicted.

Macey closed the book. The name Byron De La Beckwith was familiar. An ugly name, designed to be remembered.

Of course all the computer terminals in the media centre were busy, so she walked up and down to find somebody she could bully into letting her use theirs for a moment. Luckily Grace was working on her own project two aisles over and grumpily agreed to let Macey run an Internet search. Macey shoved herself on to half of Grace's chair and Grace muttered that their friendship was being jeopardized.

The name Byron De La Beckwith was all over the place.

In 1994 Byron De La Beckwith had finally been brought to trial. After thirty-one years, the killer of Medgar Evers went to prison.

Macey printed out a couple of pages. 'Grace?'

Grace had a habit of not speaking unless it was essential, choosing a mere lift of the eyebrows instead. This never failed to make Macey cranky. 'Don't do that, Grace. You look like a doll whose battery ran down.'

Grace giggled. 'I'm preparing for my Wall Street career. I feel sure that in high-finance circles, people do not waste time on frivolous speech when they could be making a zillion dollars that afternoon.'

'On the other hand, if you made a zillion dollars, you'd deserve a little frivolous speech.'

'OK, OK. Ask me again.'

'Grace?'

'Mace?'

They'd been doing this for years, and it still made them smile.

'You will not believe this, Grace. Austin's grand-father ordered him to order me to stop investigating.'

'I agree,' said Grace. 'Drop 1959.'

'It's got a grip on me.'

'Well, lift the wires off, like you do with your old fence,' snapped Grace. 'Macey, I'm sorry about Venita and all that, but you're getting as weird as those people who think if they find a parking space, some Greater Power made sure it was there. Some things just happen, Macey, and there's no connection. Give it a rest.'

She's right, thought Macey, I'm not resting. My mind is running around, trespassing, climbing between strands of barbed wire.

She tried to make her mind take a nap, kick off its running shoes and lie down on the sofa, but it didn't.

'I have serious bum fatigue sharing this chair with you,' said Grace. 'Get up and go away.'

Macey folded Byron De La Beckwith slowly, reading his story again, until Grace took the sheet out of Macey's hands, crushed it and threw it into one of the many wastebaskets. This room of electronic information was equally a room of wadded-up paper.

'Cut it out, Mace,' said her best friend in the softest voice Macey had ever heard her use. 'Who do you think did this anyway? You've been told! Somebody on Shell Road. And who lived on Shell Road then and who lives there now? This guy De La Beckwith goes to prison after thirty years. You want to send your own grandparents to jail? Or Austin's?'

'It wouldn't be like that,' said Macey, getting up now, giving her the whole chair. 'Mr Sibley didn't get hurt or killed, so all it really is is an old barn fire. The police wouldn't care after all these years.'

Grace stared at her. 'Then why do you care, Mace?'

That afternoon, during the long bleak stretch before her parents got home, Macey ordered her mind to lie down and take a nap, but even her body would not take a nap. She was bolt upright on the bed, surrounded by her notes and her books and the barbed wire of her thoughts. When the phone rang, she hoped it was Austin.

But it was Reverend Warren. 'Macey,' he said. His voice was very full, as if she were an entire congregation and needed strengthening.

She was so pleased to hear from him.

'The children in afternoon church care are enjoying the boxes of crayons you sent them, Macey.'

She'd spent her untouched birthday money on new crayons, worrying whether to buy the boxes with eight crayons or the boxes with twenty-four. She could afford more boxes of eight, but then that left out the really good colours. Finally she bought some of each.

She had not told her parents. Not told her grandparents. Not told Austin. She had hardly told herself.

'Did you finish painting the Sunday school rooms?' she asked him.

'We did. The colours are beautiful. The whole place sparkles. One of the Sunday school teachers bought gold paint and stencilled Venita's name in tall, thin script on the wall in the indigo room. Venita loved that word *indigo*.'

So there was a memorial. A tall slanting *V* in gleaming gold. 'I wanted to come back,' she said. 'I wanted to finish.' She could not say out loud to Reverend Warren, 'But my parents would never let me.'

And then she realized that of course he knew that.

Everybody knew. It was no secret. Macey just hadn't known yet.

He said, 'We've received a letter from the school, withdrawing the volunteers from another joint project we had scheduled. I just wanted you to know that I understand. After Venita's murder, I respect that parents aren't going to want their teenagers here.'

Macey had not even known there was another project. 'What were we going to work on?' she said.

'We're building cubby holes for the children, so they'll have their own places to hang a coat and save a paper and store crayons. You'd have nailed and glued and painted.'

Grace is right, thought Macey. Who cares about 1959? There are cubby holes to build in 1997. My colours are still not-thinking colours.

Austin's grandparents headed off to bed at nine o'clock. Aus could not fathom going to bed so early. He yearned for college dorms and all-nighters. He picked up the phone book, found Vinnie Raspardo, and called the man who had been fire chief in 1959.

'Mr Raspardo, sir,' he said, 'I'm doing a high-school project, and I'm looking into the fire on Shell Road in December of 1959 in which a teacher named Wade Sibley lost his house. Can you tell me anything about that fire?'

There was a long pause. 'I'm eighty-three, son. The old brain just doesn't compute the way it used to. Now say all that again for me.'

Austin said it all again for him. This time he included a one-word description of Wade Sibley.

'It sounds familiar, son. But those old fires just blend in, you can't keep 'em straight all these years later.'

Austin did not believe this pleasant town had had enough arson over the years that the fire chief could not keep the incidents straight. Surely only one arson had involved a man as unique as Wade Sibley. The one word – *black* – didn't often apply in this part of Connecticut.

On the other hand, eighty-three was four years older than Grandfather. Perhaps eighty-three was allowed to be forgetful. 'Are there fire department files I could read?'

'No. This is just a local volunteer setup. Forty years ago, it was pretty loose. We kept records, but they didn't have much detail, and we didn't keep them long.' Mr Raspardo did not sound forgetful on the subject of written records.

'Who else might have gone to the fire who'd remember it?'

'Nobody alive.'

'Was there a fire marshal? Would there be separate files in some other department?' asked Austin.

'Would have been once, but that's the state, not the town, and there again, son, it's too long ago. They'd never keep things forty years.'

So there is no proof, thought Austin, and there never will be.

Sunday was warm and sunny. Summer chores loomed suddenly, as if they'd run out from behind the house.

Austin and his grandfather were considering exactly how to rebuild the old stone wall. Over the years it had slumped, letting poison ivy and briar rose grow up among the fallen rocks. They were going to remove the entire wall, grub out roots, dig a ditch for a good gravel base and then replace each stone.

145

The stones had gathered heat from the sun. Austin loved handling them, loved his own strength, lifting such heavy rocks. It was a task where he could not go wrong. It would be hard, and yet it would fall into place. He'd chalk each stone, so that in replacing them, he'd make the same choices as the original mason, stacking that stone on this one, balancing that extra-crooked stone with this slender slab. Macey would bring him cookies fresh out of the oven, and real lemonade.

He stood in the shade of new leaves and surveyed the houses on Shell Road. Beautiful houses: mansions, really. Beautiful yards: display gardens, really. Everything swept, manicured, pruned, arranged. Every porch freshly painted, every windowpane scrubbed.

He thought of a man who probably had just wanted to bake a potato for dinner and work on a lesson plan for the next day. But there was no trace left of Wade Sibley. He was history.

Aus had an odd shaft of thought, like sunlight through a cloud: His parents were also history.

When the going got rough, thought Aus, I packed my bags and left town. They didn't throw me out. I basically said, Hey, you two, I'm not in this for the long haul; you guys bicker and I'm out of here. You fall on hard times and I bail.

Grandfather measured a reasonable distance to move the stones, leaving working room for shovels and the sled for towing the stones. They didn't want to haul those stones one inch farther than they had to.

The warmth of the sun seemed unearned, as if he should be standing in arctic cold, bitten by the wind. It had not crossed Austin's mind that *he* was the one who had failed. His fingers tightened on the rock he held. He wanted to pound it until stone dust flew and chips fell.

Labour, as always, distracted Aus. There was nothing like sweat to make you forget your problems. Or who caused them.

'Grandfather,' he said, sweating hard after shifting only a few feet of wall, 'you can't do this with me. You throw your back out, you'll really be in trouble.'

His grandfather hated being reminded that he was old. 'Take you all summer if you do it alone,' said Grandfather grumpily. 'In July, when it's eighty-five degrees and a hundred per cent humidity, it's not going to be fun.'

And Macey came running over, shouting hello, two sheets of white paper and an envelope in her hand. It tickled Austin the way she lived in an elementary-school, show-and-tell world, backing up her stories with objects.

She didn't slow down as she ran towards them, and Austin thought, She's running straight at me! and he managed to set the stone back down before she flung herself on him, giving him the hug of his life and a casual 'Hi, Mr Fent, how are you?' to Grandfather. If this was the result he was going to get from stone walls, he would skip college; he would be a mason; he would live among bricks and rocks.

'What's so funny?' said Macey.

He hugged her back, laughing, because it was easy and comfortable.

'I got a letter from Bonnie's mother,' said Macey.

'Isn't that amazing? This story has been lying here all these years. We forgot it, but other people didn't.' She handed him the letter, and Austin braced himself.

Sure enough: 'What story is that, Macey?' said Grandfather pleasantly.

Macey gave him a sweet smile. The sun glinted on her dark hair – two inches long now. 'Because of the fire I was in, Mr Fent, I got interested in the arson in the old barn. It's my topic for the history paper. Aus did tell me you wanted me to stop. But that isn't possible.'

Grandfather blinked once. Then he continued measuring the wall.

Aus read Bonnie's mother's letter out loud.

'"I was president of the PTA in 1959. We had many angry parents. They were appalled that a Negro had been hired. They wanted their children transferred out of his classes. But they did not want to say so publicly. They were sure that they were good people, you see, unlike the nasty people in Arkansas and Mississippi. But it's easier to be good when you are not tested, and Mr Sibley was a test, and parents failed. They did not want a coloured person in town.

There was an English teacher. Her name was Miss McCune. She was elderly at the time and could not possibly still be alive. Teaching poetry was her life. She taught beauty; she believed that no matter what happens in the world, you still possess beauty and truth.

After the fire, she sent a poem home. It was mimeographed, that's how you made copies then. It came out blue. The children in her classes were required to memorize it. John Greenleaf Whittier's 'O Brother*

148

Man'. At the end of the poem, it says, 'Love shall tread
out the baleful fire of anger, and in its ashes plant the tree
of peace.'

I have always wanted to find out what happened to
Mr Sibley. Whether his tree of peace has grown tall and
sturdy. Or whether he is trapped in the ashes of our
burning." '

Austin pictured Miss McCune as white-haired and thin,
but strong and sure: typing her inky mimeo master-
copy; fastening it carefully on the big roller, churning
the handle, making copies one by one of the poem she
thought might teach brotherhood. It did not look as if
Miss McCune had accomplished much.

His grandfather said nothing. How powerful silence
was. Silence kept you standing exactly where you were.

Austin said to Macey, 'I called the fire chief. Vinnie
Raspardo. He can't remember the barn fire and there
are no records.'

He was sending this message to his grandfather; he
was reporting in. If you did it, Grandfather, you can
relax. It doesn't matter what Mace finds; she cannot
find proof.

But Grandfather did not react. He seemed wholly
involved with the stones, and Austin thought: Perhaps
he is. Perhaps this really does mean nothing to him.

Macey was frowning as if she were taking a quiz, a
pencil in her teeth and an answer just out of reach. The
breeze ruffled her short hair. In his mind there was a
halo of fire around that head, and smoke and terror.
Austin, too, studied stones for relief.

'Aus, could I ask you a favour?'

'Yes'

'We can't learn anything from the fire department, but maybe we can get the person who *called* the fire department.'

Austin's grandfather clicked the button on the side of his steel measuring tape and the long flat extension whacked back up into its holder. Then he headed towards the house. Austin felt every one of his grandfather's steps on his heart.

Macey pointed. 'Whoever called in the fire lived on the other side of the creek.' Brookside Drive was a stone's throw away, but by car a long and annoying drive. Between the two neighbourhoods was a tidal creek, mud-bottomed at low tide, and swirling with currents at high tide. 'Would you go with me to ask around the neighbourhood?' she said.

Grandfather reached the side door and went in, shutting it behind him.

'They'll have moved, Macey,' said Austin.

Her face fell.

'But it's worth a try,' he said quickly.

Her face lit up, and she said, 'Now?' and he loved her for being so much like his mother: Do it now, do it with passion, don't sit down!

They walked across the Demitroff property to the edge of the water. The land was high, fifteen feet above high tide, and dropped off into rocks, but at the creek, grass ran right down to the water's edge.

The tide was out. The creek ran thin. The water was probably only up to their ankles. 'Let's go,' he said, and the mudflats sucked their feet down, and gritty salt water filled his work boots. They had not walked fifty feet on the far side of the creek when they were hailed and a man called in a falsely polite voice, 'May I help you?'

Good thing we like dogs, thought Austin. The guy's got three of them.

One was a golden retriever, no worries there. Macey knelt to hug the retriever while the other dogs, less eager to see her, growled. Their master, a middle-aged man, bifocals and not much hair, spoke to the dogs and they quietened. Their names seemed to be Janet, Darlene and Donna Lee.

Macey introduced herself and Austin. 'I'm researching a fire that happened in 1959. An old barn was torched and the fire was reported by somebody living on your side of the creek.'

The man nodded, shifting dog leashes as the dogs twined around his legs. 'Sure, I remember,' he said. 'I didn't live here then, though. Had an army career. My sister was the one who reported it. You could talk to her. She lives in New Canaan now.'

New Canaan was twenty miles away. Austin would drive Macey; take a long country drive with her, wandering on curving roads, stopping for ice cream.

'I'm Pete Yinson,' the man said. 'Come on in while I get my sister's telephone number for you.'

They walked up to the very house from which the barn fire had been seen. Austin could make out a corner of the barn foundation. They weren't as far away as he'd expected. Maybe the length of a football field.

Pete Yinson glanced down at their muddy feet.

'You're worse than the dogs. I thought people outgrew wading with their shoes on by the time they were seven,' he said, smiling. They waited on the stoop while he went in to find pencil and paper. His house was very tiny and had small furniture to fit the small rooms.

His sister was Alice Yinson. An attorney, he explained. He jotted down Alice Yinson's home and office numbers.

'And are the dogs really Janet, Darlene and Donna Lee?' asked Macey. 'I never met dogs with names like that.'

'I never met a girl with a name like yours,' said Pete Yinson. 'Pretty yuppie,' he teased, still smiling.

Austin found himself looking forward to being a grown-up and getting along with old guys like Pete Yinson and his dogs Janet, Darlene and Donna Lee.

'Mr Yinson,' he said, 'would anybody else on the street remember the fire?'

'Are you kidding? People move in and out every fifteen minutes. You never get to know them. People don't respect roots any more. I'm the only native on the street.'

They shook hands. 'Thank you, sir,' said Austin. 'Sorry we trespassed.'

'You come again,' said Mr Yinson. 'I like people with roots.'

The creek was noticeably higher and harder to cross in the short time they'd been on the other side. They held hands to keep steady. When they came up on to the grass, Austin wanted to lie down and sunbathe, take off more than wet shoes. The riverbank tilted; lying down on the grass, they could be seen only by the mockingbirds singing so joyfully in the trees.

But Macey wanted to call Alice Yinson right away.

'I could drive us to New Canaan,' Austin offered.

But she was not interested in wasting that much time. Like Austin's mother, she was headed in her direction, and he could tag along or get lost; it was up to him.

'Wade Sibley?' said Alice Yinson. 'I taught in the junior high with him.'

'You did!' cried Macey. 'What did you teach?'

'Home economics. Back then, every girl had to learn sewing and cooking and domestic skills. Naturally, later on I went back to school and took other degrees. I've been an attorney for twenty years.'

Macey talked on the wall phone while Aus listened in on the cordless. 'How wonderful,' said Macey. 'And Mr Sibley . . .'

'Taught science. Along with my first husband. His name was Adam Devers. I've had three marriages, took the man's name for each, but now I'm using my maiden name again. If I get married a fourth time, I'll keep Yinson.'

Austin hoped that neither of his parents was ever that casual about their marriage. He hoped they wanted one marriage and were at this instant putting it back together.

He knew they weren't.

Macey nodded and smiled and encouraged, as if she and Alice Yinson were sitting across from each other in a restaurant.

She still got sparks for you, Texas.

But what if his parents became strangers? What if they built new lives without him? What if they came to important decisions, and he didn't know and wasn't there?

The crazier he felt about Macey, the more he needed to go home and see what could be salvaged of his family.

Macey knew the buttons to push with sister Alice. 'And you grew up right here, didn't you?' said Macey. 'Me too. I'm a native. My grandparents were born here, too. Still live here.'

Alice Yinson warmed. 'Adam and I really wanted to teach in the town where we were born and grew up, but I can't tell you how difficult it was getting jobs.'

Austin heard what Alice Yinson did not say out loud: it was hard to get a job because the school board went and hired people from out of town. Black ones.

He had not known silence was a weapon until this afternoon. *We won't talk, and it won't exist. If the subject isn't mentioned, it doesn't count.*

Connecticut and Shell Road had mastered the weapon well. Silence was as necessary as proper clothing or good grades.

How to make people uncomfortable: bring up race. People wanted to sit someplace else and wait till you came to your senses. He was as silent as the rest. Had he talked to anyone about Isaiah, Venita, Good Shepherd? No. Because the beginner friendships he had here would not stand up to the test of the world's least acceptable topic: how do black and white kids get along?

Or don't they?

'We were a very friendly faculty,' said Alice Yinson, 'and Wade Sibley was welcomed with open arms.'

'I'm so glad to hear it,' said Macey. 'What was Mr Sibley like?'

'I hardly remember. He was there only one year, you see, and home economics was not in the same wing as science.'

'Did Mr Devers share a science lab with Mr Sibley?' asked Macey.

'Yes. Shared a desk, too.'

'Can we reach Mr Devers?' asked Macey.

'We didn't divorce. He died.'

'I'm so sorry,' said Macey.

'Don't be. It was umpty-ump years ago, and I've had two husbands since.'

Austin was finding this woman unbearable.

Macey said, 'Your brother Pete told me you called in the fire.'

'Oh, my goodness, the fire. I haven't thought of that in years.'

Here it was again. How many times in your life did you phone in an arson? The fire *had* to have been the first thing that came to Alice Yinson's mind.

'You could see the barn clearly from your house, couldn't you?' said Macey.

'Oh, yes. I'd been in the barn apartment, actually. Lovely little place.'

'Tell me about it,' said Macey in a cuddly, feminine voice Austin could never have duplicated.

'It had this charming sitting room, open to the

rafters, and the curtains were bright red, and the rugs too, and the sun came up and filled the place with light. The kitchen was just darling, tall, thin white cabinets and little handles shaped like apples. The dining table was pushed up against the window, with a beautiful view of the yacht club.'

How could she remember the apartment so well and not remember Mr Sibley? thought Austin. But then, women seemed to care more about stuff like pillows and pictures. It was another of his parents' problems. Dad failed to notice anything in the way of a scented candle or new dried flowers. He certainly failed to understand why hard-earned money should be spent on them. Mom shrieked that he might as well be a hound dog sleeping on an old blanket in the garage. Dad yelled that . . . oh, well.

'Nobody could believe that the owners would . . . um . . .' Alice Yinson coughed.

Austin knew the rest of the sentence. Nobody could believe that the owners rented to a black man instead of me, Alice Yinson Devers. Homemaker and native of the town.

I'm no different from this awful woman, he thought. I couldn't believe I was trapped in that fire. I didn't deserve it. Not me. Not rich, white Austin.

Alice finished coughing. 'My husband and I were living with my parents that year,' she said, 'and just happened to look up and see flames across the brook. We telephoned the fire department. Back then you didn't have 911, you know. You had to look up the phone number like any other number.'

156

Austin made a resolution. When he got married, he would not live with his in-laws in a little teeny house with little teeny furniture and spend his time gazing at the apartment he had not got.

'Did you go see the fire?' asked Macey.

'No. That brook is dangerous at high tide.'

It was 1959, not 1659, thought Austin. You could have got in the car and driven over, like everybody else who was curious.

But Alice got to that. 'We were not the kind of people who drive to fires and clutter the roads, gawking at the misfortunes of others. I'm sorry, Miss Clare, but I have a client waiting. Good luck on your project.' She hung up.

Macey put her phone down sadly. 'Oh, Aus! What was it like for Mr Sibley? If that woman was welcoming, he must have felt as if he were living in a freezer.'

They hugged to find the warmth Mr Sibley had not received. It was a quick, neighbourly hug. Austin did not want to be neighbours with Macey. But that's what this is about, he thought. Neighbours, and what they are.

'Mace,' he said, and he could hardly swallow, hardly think. He absolutely could not talk about Mr Sibley another minute. He could not think about Miss McCune's poem, or divorce, or parents or grandparents. 'Let's go to a movie tonight.'

She smiled as if he were a prince, the kind who carved marshmallow sticks, the kind whose T-shirt would hang for ever in the back porch of their memories. 'Yes. Let's.'

9

Mrs Johnson had forced a local history project upon Aus. She stuck him with railroads. He would just as soon lie down on the tracks as waste his time researching railroads in Connecticut. Every time he thought about it, he went into a coma, or else had to go outside and shift some stone wall. So far he had not collected a single fact about railroads in Connecticut. The month of May was rushing right along, and soon the project would be due.

But his first date with Macey had left him giddy and light of heart.

He wanted to scrap all events unrelated to Macey and throw himself into all things that touched her. So railroads were stupid and pointless, but 1959 was interesting after all.

'I want to pry into somebody's life, Graff,' said Austin. 'Are there books on how to do that?'

'Very popular hobby,' said Graff, handing him two books.

Austin checked them both out.

'Look at all this stuff that's public record!' he said to Macey, mesmerized by what he could find out about strangers. 'Things we could find on file in the Fairfield County judicial offices in Bridgeport,' he said excitedly,

'include affidavits, breach of whatever, tax rights, cert-
ificates of title, changes of name, deeds, fictious names,
judgements, powers of attorney, pet licences!'

'Did Mr Sibley have any of those?' she said
dubiously. 'And if they didn't save records from voting,
are they going to save pet licences? Come on, Aus.'

They were sitting on the carpet in the hall outside
the media centre. Theirs was a school of hall sitters, so
that many pairs of legs stuck out on both sides, making
the usable corridor very narrow, unless you ran down
the hall, leaping over legs like a high jumper. Macey
and Austin ignored the treads and heels that passed
airborne over their flat knees.

'What we need to go after,' said Austin, 'is driving
history. We send in his date of birth and twenty-five
dollars, and we get Wade Sibley's driving history.'

'We can't do that.'

'Sure we can. It's right in the book.' He waved the
instructions at her. Of course, they didn't have his date
of birth, but Wade Sibley was an unusual name, they
knew Mr Sibley was twenty-two in 1959, and a decent
computer program would accept parameters.

'It's sly,' she said. 'It's sneaky. It's peeking into his
life where we have no business looking.'

'No, it isn't. This is public information. We're the
public.'

'But *he* isn't public, Aus. Anyway, why would we
want his driving history?'

'We want something! We don't have anything. He's
the only person who knows what really happened, so if
you truly want to find out, Mace, you have to find Mr

Sibley. It says his driving history will include his social security number. I don't know much, but I know that with a social security number, you can really zip into people's private lives.'

They were very close, but not touching. Air space ran from their shoulders to their thighs to their ankles. Austin looked down at the air space. The more he looked, the more important it got. He shifted over to fill the inch. She looked at him. The angle was awkward, so he slumped down until their noses were even. Very lightly, he touched the tip of her nose with the tip of his. Very lightly, she pressed her cheek against his.

For a moment, his entire world was skin against skin.

But this was high school, where nothing was private, and in any case, they had not chosen a private location. 'Go, Aus!' said one of his friends, kicking the sole of Austin's shoe. From farther down the line of hall sitters came a long high whistle.

Macey pulled back, as he had known she would. Acting as if nothing had happened, she dragged her bag on to her lap, where Austin would have liked to be, and took out a plastic bag. She gave Austin two of what might have been the world's best chocolate chip oatmeal raisin cookies, although he personally preferred them without the oatmeal and the raisins.

'Aus, it isn't Mr Sibley's private life I want to zip into. It's the fire.'

He was on fire himself. Only a week ago, he had been sure of a lot of things, and now he was sure of nothing, except that all time spent with Macey was good time.

'People burned his house down around him, Aus,' said Macey, nibbling around the edge of her cookie as if it were an ear of corn. 'I can't be the next generation and pry around the edges of his life, like some second burn.'

'You aren't prying,' said Austin. 'You're trying to find the guy. This is a legal and business-like approach.'

'I don't know, Aus. It's hard for me to feel 1959. I try to touch it, and it moves away. It feels like a slower time, an easier time . . . and yet such a dim, shadowy time.'

'That's because you're trying to find out what it was like to be black in 1959, and you're never going to know that,' said Austin. 'The only thing we might figure out is what it was like to be white in 1959.' Aus felt like weather: he was a warm front, she was a cold front, and any moment there would be a storm. When he touched his cheek against hers, pressure began to build that Austin could not manage. 'OK, fine, we won't trace the guy through his driving records,' said Austin. 'Let's go to the old junior high and interview teachers who were there in 1959.'

'Aus,' she said, 'you're a genius.'

Austin jumped to his feet, stuck his hand down and pulled her up.

When Mr Sibley taught, the building had been a junior high, grades seven through nine, but now it was a middle school, six through eight.

Middle school was not a phase of life that Macey cared to recall. In seventh grade, she had grown tall so quickly that her arms and legs did not match. She fell off platforms when the choir sang. Stairways tripped her going up and ambushed her going down. When she clapped, her palms missed, because one arm was longer than the other. Her parents took her to the doctor, who said that was ridiculous, her arms matched fine – but what did he know? She was the one whose hands missed when she tried to clap.

How had it been here for Mr Sibley? Had he been on tiptoe, as Dr King had written? Harried by day and haunted by night? Or was he just teaching and never thought about it? After the fire, he sure thought about it.

A teacher Macey had never had, a woman so old she must have been around thirty-eight years ago, trudged wearily towards them. 'Mrs Smith!' Macey called, trotting over.

Mrs Smith smiled in the bright, unremembering way of people who see thousands of kids over the years.

'My name is Macey Clare. I was here a few years ago, but you weren't one of my teachers.'

Mrs Smith continued trudging, and Macey fell in step. 'I'm hoping to talk to a teacher or an administrator who was here in 1959. Were you?'

'No, I didn't go back to work till after my children were grown. That was seventy-nine. I don't think there's a single person here who taught here in fifty-nine. The principal would have been Bob Rutland, and he's been dead twenty years.' She said this while still walking, and by the time her sentences were done, she had entered a classroom, and Macey and Aus were alone in the hall with her echo.

162

Mr Sibley was not even an echo.

They left the middle school. Macey headed for the first shortcut towards Nana and Papa's.

'No. I'm starving,' said Austin. He took her shoulders and rerouted her. 'We don't want asparagus omelettes,' he said firmly. 'We want Big Macs.'

McDonald's was a familiar and public as the hall at school.

They did not touch cheeks. They did not sit next to each other, but facing.

They had hot salty french fries, and thick slurpy milk shakes, and burgers with bacon and lettuce and tomato and cheese.

Macey was as happy as she had ever been in her life.

Sparks flew, but they were not in a place where anything could catch fire.

It did not matter. It was spring, and they had homes across the street, a summer to come, and time in the sun.

On Saturday Macey and her parents toured garden centres. It was always this way: in early May, Mom and Dad were sure this was the year they would garden, and weed, and tend, and their yard would yield armloads of dizzyingly bright flowers, and there would be pretty little paths edged by fragrant herbs.

But somehow, once they got home, everybody was too busy actually to plant anything, and the plants would line up near the garage in the sun, waiting for a shovel and a space in the earth, but the time wouldn't come and a few weeks later somebody would irritably fork the silly things into a corner, and Mom would say, Next year, I think I'll plant roses.

Macey especially loved her parents when they just foozled around and got nowhere but wouldn't admit it.

On the drive home, Dad said, 'Do we need to stop for anything?' He hated getting up Sunday morning and finding they were out of milk or coffee or orange juice.

'We'd better stop just in case,' agreed Mom.

Dad pulled up to the convenience store. 'Mace, you know you want to run into the store for us.'

'Sure,' she said, because she did want to. She liked helping keep her parents' lives together.

'I think we're out of cereal, Macey,' said Mom. 'Get Cheerios too.'

She handed Macey a twenty, and Macey ran in, knowing the aisles well, pulling milk out of the refrigerated doors and cereal off the shelf. She got doughnuts too. Sunday morning you needed a doughnut. She was back in moments. She hopped in, slammed the door, and showed off her loot. Everybody was happy about the doughnuts, especially Mom, who would never have bought them but would be the first to eat them.

Her parents mentioned what a good mood she was in, how happy she seemed. Macey said, 'Oh, you know. Spring. Sun is shining.'

They believed her. They actually thought she was dancing around the marigolds because she liked marigolds. This made Macey burst out laughing and think of Monday, and think of Austin in school on Monday.

As soon as they got home, she e-mailed Lindsay. 'Linz,' she typed, because this was Lindsay's e-mail address, 'I went to Mackey D's with Aus. Shared a large fry. Used the same squirt of ketchup. Is this romance or what?'

Lindsay checked her mail constantly, crushed and grieving if there were not lots of communications, so she answered an hour later. 'No. It is not romance. You must improve your standards. There's a wonderful article in *Seventeen Magazine* I could download and e-mail Aus. Then he'd have some clues on how to date.'

Luckily there was time to respond to this. 'Don't even think about it, Linz. Death comes to those who interfere in other people's love lives.'

Then she phoned Grace and they talked for a while about love lives and how incredibly wonderful it was that she, Macey Clare, possessed one.

She felt as warm and soft as a cake just out of the oven.

There was a boy next door and he was perfect.

Austin called his mother.

She could not have been more hostile and dis-agreeable.

He felt bludgeoned by her anger.

Aus tried not to be hostile back. The giddy pleasure of being with Macey evaporated. When other topics failed, he said, 'Mom, I need to know more about that fire. In 1959.'

'Oh, Austin!' she said. 'I was little, OK? I don't know the facts. Ask Macey's mother.'

'She won't talk about it. I need you to tell me what you think happened.'

'OK, fine!' she snapped. 'Somebody on Shell Road decided enough was enough. They didn't want a black man living there. They torched the place.'

Every one of his worries returned, dark and terrible. He could not believe he had actually encouraged Macey to return to the barn fire. He could not believe he had jumped in to help her get closer to the facts. He said sadly, 'Was it Grandfather?'

'Henry Fent is discussing this with you?' said his mother, anger replaced by astonishment. She often referred to her father by name, as if they were not related.

'No, Mom. He told me to stop looking into it.'

There was a long pause. His mother said, 'It doesn't matter whether or not Henry Fent started that fire. He's guilty.'

'What do you mean?' said Austin. 'In a court of law is what I mean.'

'I mean in a court of God,' said his mother.

Austin was facing the window as he spoke, and beyond him stretched sea and sky, darkening into night, no star and no comet visible. A court of God? Where, and what, was that?

'You could at least call to ask how I am, Austin,' she said, 'instead of harking back forty years. I'd like to know why you're living there and not with me or your father! Have you lost interest in me completely?'

'No, Mom,' he said desperately.

'As your father has lost interest in me.'

166

'Mom, he hasn't lost interest, he just doesn't know what to do next.'

'And about our last phone call. I'd like to know why you hang up on your own mother. I'd like to know just what kind of son you are.'

He really was very like his father. He could not frame his questions and answers as quickly as she could. His mind was stumbling with this conversation, and he took too long. She was the one to hang up without saying goodbye.

His eyes stung. When I have children of my own, he thought – and he had never thought about his future children, the possibility of them, but now he thought of them – when I have children of my own, they will not have to call me up, because I will already be there.

What made his mother so terribly angry? It could not have anything to do with the history of Shell Road. And it could not have anything to do with Henry and Monica Fent, because Mom's relationship with her parents had always been infrequent and strained.

He did not want his relationship with his parents to be infrequent and strained.

He felt as if the last few days with Macey had been a balloon, shining and soaring – and temporary.

Like a little kid after a bad day in kindergarten, all he wanted was to go home.

Monday spun Macey around.

There was a boy next door and they were in love.

Of course, then she didn't see Aus the entire morning. She hardly minded. It meant the school was waiting, as she was: down some hall, behind some classroom door, it was keeping Austin for her.

Macey finally spotted him after lunch and yelled, 'Aus!' at his broad back. He was wearing a long-sleeved shirt with a hand collar, soft faded blue stripes with that J. Crew look, and she thought, Pretty soon I'll have his clothes memorized; I wonder if he'll have mine memorized. She yelled, 'Aus!' again, and he half turned and waved, but walked on.

She ran after him. 'Hi, Aus,' she said.

He nodded at her with a sort of tight-lipped recognition. 'Hey, Mace.'

She fell in step with him.

He didn't say anything.

She thought I should have worn different clothes. I should have put on makeup.

'I called my dad,' he said. 'I might just head on back to Chicago.'

'*What?*' He was thinking of home? He never mentioned home! It meant nothing to him. He'd written it off. 'But – but – Aus . . .' She couldn't think. She was out of breath and out of brain. What about summer? What good would summer be if Aus went home? What good would anything be? She had thought – she was sure—

'There's only three more weeks of school, Aus,' she said. 'You can't go home now.' She did not want him to go home ever. She wanted his home to be here, not there.

He shrugged. 'I can take finals at my old high school. They'd mail the tests and supervise me there.'

Macey had to make him stop walking, as if she didn't matter. 'Aus,' she said, 'I've decided that what we need to do next is find the Beedons. The ones who took Mr Sibley in. We know they lived in that red house on the hill above the baseball field. So let's go to the town library after school, and from the 1959 city directory, we can find their full name and how to spell it and then—'

'Mace, you're going to have to count me out.' He shifted his books in front of him. 'See you,' he said, walking on.

High schools did not have hideaways. There was no designated refuge. There was no corner in which you could vanish. You could not sign up to be tutored instead, sparing yourself twenty classmates.

The teacher was reviewing for a test, and Macey cared intensely about every test everywhere, but she had not known there was a test with Austin.

He still likes me, she told herself. She felt like a collection of body parts being flung around the room. His grandfather came down on him. He had to back away from the research. He isn't counting himself out because of me.

You got a crush on that boy? That one named for Texas?

Her breathing came so short and quick that the act of taking in air was exhausting.

He's your man, whether him and you want it or not.

But Austin did not want.

It's my fault, she thought. I dragged us into family-wrecking stuff when I should have been thinking about him.

169

When school ended, Macey did not want to leave the building. She did not want to sit in an empty house for four hours before Mom and Dad got back. She certainly did not want to go to Nana and Papa's and risk seeing Austin.

Oh, Austin. How could you want to go home?

If I hadn't gone where Austin's grandfather told me not to go, she thought, everything here would have stayed sunny and bright, and Aus would have wanted his summer plans more than his parents.

Macey had expected to be the summer plans.

She took refuge in the media centre. For an hour after school it was an unofficial computer club, kids drifting in and out, sending e-mail, surfing the Web. People didn't bother you when you were on the computer. It was a public activity that gave you privacy.

Graff and Mrs Johnson were circling, helping people who were at the last stages of despair, with no hope of finishing their projects.

Macey's chief occupation was not to cry. Her second occupation was to look busy enough so nobody would interrupt her.

She fiddled mindlessly, eventually typing in the address she knew best right now: the local newspaper. She scrolled down their home page and there, way at the bottom, where she thought she'd been, but obviously not, Macey discovered an online obituary file.

Who did she know who was dead?

She cringed at this sentence, but – the last dead guy she had talked about was Adam Devers, several husbands ago for Alice Yinson. Macey typed. Waited.

Pages began to form. There was something so neat about the Net: facts slowly painting themselves out of the unknown.

Mr Devers had died by his own hand, in November 1960.

Macey shut down the computer without getting out of Netscape and thought, Great, I probably crashed it, nobody'll ever be able to use it again. And who would want to?

She sat staring at nothing, until finally Mrs Johnson was available. She forced every other thought out of her mind; forced away the presence of Aus.

'Mrs Johnson, remember that I got interested in the very first black teacher ever hired here? And people wanted him out of here, so they burned his home down around him to make him go?'

'Macey,' interrupted Mrs Johnson, upset, 'that kind of thing never happened here.'

'That's what everybody says. But it isn't true. Listen to me. Please listen.'

Mrs Johnson didn't sit down to listen to Mr Sibley's story. She didn't look at Macey and listen. She didn't stop what she was doing to listen. She went right on checking off a list of students whose outlines and progress she had not yet seen.

Macey wanted Mr Sibley to have undivided attention. With nobody listening, the story dwindled down to a few sentences, which weren't gripping because there was nobody to grip.

'Mace,' said Mrs. Johnson at last, 'what do you think you're doing – scripting a television series? You can't write a paper that's nothing but neighbourhood gossip. This is not research, Macey. This is very unattractive rumour spreading.'

A terrible anger, born against Aus but impossible to use against him, began rising in Macey. 'Mrs Johnson,' she said. 'In one of my books, I read how even libraries were segregated. In the South, they didn't lend white people's books to people whose black skin might rub off on the page.'

'Well, that's the South. You expected that kind of thing there. But we—'

'Everybody keeps saying we were so civilized, we never did anything ugly. But we did. Right here. We don't have a halo!'

Mrs Johnson shook her head. 'Macey, look at this 1959 newspaper clipping you photocopied. It doesn't even mention this teacher. It does not say arson.' Mrs Johnson turned to the next kid waiting. 'Josh. Where's your outline?'

Austin had not called his father.

He had planned the call, he had imagined the call, he had even rehearsed the call. But he had not made the call.

He had considered returning to his old high school. He'd taken imaginary final exams in the principal's office in Chicago. He'd got imaginary extremely high grades.

But he was here, in this house, with Grandmother and Grandfather.

It was Monday evening, and if Dad ever called, it was Monday. Austin hung around the phone like a little kid.

Austin was amazed by how much he loved his grandmother and his grandfather. He was amazed by how deeply it wrenched him that these two might have planned and executed an arson, expecting the man inside to burn to death.

I can pretend it isn't them, he thought.

But he had decided not to pretend that his mother and father loved him, and he did not want to pretend that Grandmother and Grandfather were good people if they weren't.

He ached for talk; he wanted to talk all night; he wanted to hear his own voice turning over every possibility, finding every escape route; he wanted to come up with a truth that did not include arson or grandparents.

He was sick with thinking about Macey. He wanted to escape that too.

And maybe even escape Macey.

He thought of the Beedons, who had vanished into time. Macey would have hunted them down this afternoon, without him. What had made them get in the car and drive down Shell Road to help Wade Sibley? Had Mr Sibley been glad to see them? Or angry that he, a grown man, needed rescue? Had he felt like a child, climbing into the back seat of their car, taken home to be fed and dressed? Or was he just glad to have friends?

And then Dad called.

'Hi!' said Austin. He was embarrassed at how glad he was to hear his father's voice. 'How are you?' he said eagerly.

'OK. Not great. How are you?'

He wanted to be in the same room with his father.

He wanted to see his father's face, and if Dad had given up smoking again that day, and whether he was wearing the old grey sweatsuit he usually hung out in.

'Ok, Dad.'

The conversation stalled.

They had never run out of things to say when they lived together. It was the phone that did it. Austin was completely at ease on the phone – except with this stranger, his father, who had left that other stranger, his mother. Austin said, 'Dad, Macey and I have been researching this project.'

'Who?' said his father.

His father did not know Macey. It seemed impossible.

But then, Dad never stayed the whole month of July, when Austin and Mom visited. Dad hardly stayed more than a weekend. He wasn't fond of his in-laws.

'You know Macey's grandparents,' said Austin. 'Putnam and Leandra Macey, they live on the other side of Shell Road from Grandmother and Grandfather? Macey's mother is Cordelia Clare? And their daughter was named Macey for that side of the family?'

'Oh, right. Little girl. Dark eyes. About ten.'

'Well, she probably was ten when you saw her last, Dad, but now she's almost sixteen. Macey stumbled on an ancient crime, Dad. An arson. It was committed December fourth, 1959, and it was the burning of a barn apartment on Shell Road.' His voice was giving way. 'The apartment was occupied by the first black teacher in town, and the fire was started to drive him away, and maybe to kill him.'

'That's horrible, Aus,' said his father. 'I never heard about that. Where was this barn?'

Austin told him the piling up of half facts and half guesses, but long before he got to whether Grandfather started the fire, long before he quoted Mom (it doesn't matter if your grandfather started the fire; he's guilty), Austin spilled the truth of his own fire. Venita, Isaiah, Davonn, Chamique, Macey, Lindsay, Grace. *Hamlet*. The Church of the Good Shepherd. Macey's hair in flames. His T-shirt smothering and saving her. The lies they'd agreed to tell and the reasons they'd agreed to tell them. Venita's murder. Dorothy Edna Loomis's letter. Macey. Helping her research something he knew perfectly well they should not be researching.

'You went through that without me?' said his father, stunned. 'Oh, Aus. I've been such a lousy parent. I'm sorry, Aus.'

'Dad,' said Austin, 'when do I come home? What's going on? What are you and Mom doing? Where is everybody going to live? Grandfather and I had a lot of plans for the summer, Dad, and . . . but . . .' He felt shaky, as if he hadn't eaten for days. 'What's happening, Dad?'

It was not slang, that 'What's happening?' It was his heart.

His father said, 'How about if I fly in this weekend and visit, and you and I'll talk?'

'Yes,' said Austin, and he was rattled that Dad was going to come to Connecticut instead of having Austin go to Chicago. It sounded bad, very bad, and yet he wanted his father here. He said, 'Dad, I talked to Mom yesterday, and she's so angry with me. I didn't do anything.'

'You forgot her birthday and Mother's Day.'

'Oh, no! When were they?'

'May sixth and May eleventh. I should have called to remind you.' His father sighed. 'There are about a million things I should have done.'

Austin was strangely cheered. Mom hadn't forgotten him; she was hurt. This sounded like something he could solve, or at least wire flowers.

He could hardly bear to say goodbye to his father. The stretch to Friday seemed like years.

Well, he would make use of the rest of the week.

He and his father had left the 1959 story and entered their own. But the truth of 1959 was out there, and now Austin needed it too, as much as Macey did.

He reached for a photocopy he'd made of one of Macey's pages.

Then he picked up the phone.

Austin is leaving.

Macey took the late bus home, listening to the babble around her. Normally she loved other people's conversations. Today they sounded like ducks quacking.

Austin is leaving.

She made it to the house without breaking down.

She got stranded in the front hall. There seemed no point in going farther.

Macey stared at the wallpaper pattern. It was pale lemon yellow, sparkling with dark gold antique suns and silver rays from shooting stars. It repeated every few feet, so you could follow the stars around the room, like a galaxy.

She could not bear to turn on the television in order to warm herself in front of a fake family.

Austin is leaving.

It was six-fifteen. Still one more hour before her parents got home.

You got kids their moms never home and they burn theirselves in spaghetti water.

Oh, Venita! she thought, feeling physical pain. I didn't want to have that in common with you.

She got on her bike and rode to Nana and Papa's. Nana was making dessert, of course, layers of raspberries and white cake and chocolate drizzle and dollops of sweet whipped cream. All the lovely waiting was what Nana loved about cooking. And what had Nana waited for in the middle of the night on December 4, 1959?

'Whip the cream for me, darling,' said Nana.

Macey obeyed. The big countertop mixer whipped by itself while Macey watched the bowl turn. Even though I told Aus that I don't believe things are meant, I did believe he was meant. Meant for me. Grace and I agreed on that. I believed I had all kinds of time, because it was meant, because Texas was proud of saving me, and we would be together for always.

But Stella Miller knew the truth. You have to play your cards right in this world. I didn't play my cards right.

When the kitchen phone rang, she was closest.

'Mace,' said Austin.

'Hi.' She was completely surprised. She had nothing to say. She might go and cry, right here in the kitchen in front of Nana and Papa.

'I called those other people,' he said.

Other people?

'The ones that still live in town even though they don't live on Shell Road any more. Remember there were a bunch more we never got to?'

They were back at Mr Sibley. Macey didn't want to be in 1959. She wanted to be in Austin's hug.

Aus said, 'I called the first person. No recollection. I called the second person. No recollection. I called the third person. They have photographs.'

'Photographs?' repeated Macey.

'Of the fire. They were there, they brought their camera, they still have the photographs.'

10

There were seven photographs.

Black and white.

The first photograph showed flames shooting up beyond the top of the picture. Macey would not have known there was a building. It was all fire.

The second was not centred. Winter-bare branches were silhouetted against a moonlit sky, and off to the side blazed a roof of fire.

The third and fourth photographs were fire trucks and firemen, aiming a hose so large that several men grappled to control it.

The fifth was strangely beautiful: from a distant, invisible hose came a silver waterfall arching over smoking ruins.

In the sixth, the fire had burned out, but barn timber still stood. A single window frame still hung in position. A side wall had burned irregularly, turning into a char-red picket fence. Within this skeleton, a car was a coagulated knot of melted metal.

That was the photograph that left no doubt. It had been a fire planned to kill.

Macey touched her short hair and remembered the taste of fire. She turned the album page to the seventh photograph. It showed neighbours standing in a row, arms folded, watching.

Macey could tell from a single white pillar and the edge of a porch rail that they were lined up in front of her grandparents' house. Her grandfather and grandmother; Austin's grandfather; three men she could not identify; and one woman.

Macey had not just been reading about 1959. She had also read about arson. People who purposely set fires came back to admire their work. So this row of people – were they admiring their work?

Austin had said that the men at the beach bonfire were like ancient priests setting a sacrificial fire. Had this row of people chosen the victim for 1959?

Austin said, 'I'm really interested, sir, that you saved the photographs.'

Mr Collins was very old and very gnarled. His strength and beauty had vanished into old age, and if he had been an athlete or a star, it didn't show. He was just old in the scary, stale way nobody ever wanted to be. Mr Collins said, 'It was a bad night. I still remember it.'

Mr Collins had been a neighbour in a small house sold years ago, the house worth nothing compared to the land, his house pulled down and a mansion put in its place. Now he lived in a tiny brick slice of an apartment, with a single flower in a pot on the step.

'And the renter from the apartment?' said Macey. 'The owner of that burned-up car? Where was he? There isn't a photograph of him.'

'The guy was a Negro. I remember how astonished we were, the wife and me. A coloured man in that part of town? I mean, there was a project where a few of 'em lived then, and maybe there were one or two families renting above stores on the avenue, but Shell Road? It would be amazing to see a black family there *now*, but then? I remember the wife saying he must be yard help, but no. He lived there.'

'Did you meet him?' asked Macey.

'Didn't talk to him. He was wearing pyjamas. I remember that. That's how I realized the guy really did live there.'

'May I borrow your photographs?' asked Macey.

He slid one finger behind each photograph, lifting them from the four little black triangles that held them against the black page of his album. 'You can have them.' Mr Collins found a sandwich bag and slid the photographs into it.

'What happened when everybody went home?' asked Aus. 'Did somebody take the teacher in for the night?'

'The Beedons,' said Mr Collins. 'Nice couple.' He looked shyly at Austin and Macey. 'The wife and I talked about it. The guy had no home, no nothing. We thought we'd call the minister, see if he knew a place the guy could stay, and then we thought, well, we have an extra room, the girls are grown. But we weren't sure, we needed time to think, it was a big step, and then the Beedons drove up.'

'Did Mr Sibley know the Beedons?' said Macey.

'No idea.'

'Do you know where the Beedons moved?' asked Macey. 'Where they are now?'

'No idea.'

*

181

Grandfather bought his cars by the pound. The longer and heavier they were, the more he respected them. This was a Lincoln, more of a sofa with an engine than a car. Tonight was the first time Austin's grandfather had let him take the Lincoln out after dark by himself.

Shell Road was south of the interstate motorway, the railroad and the town. It peeled quietly away from the main roads and crept beneath low-hanging limbs of maple and oak. It wound between old stone walls, avoiding the ravine and the creek. It was narrow, with no shoulder and no pavement. It had no streetlights. Trees were a religion here; every house must be dwarfed by its trees, embraced by its shrubs.

Aus had rolled his window down, and it was lilac time, so as they coasted towards the end of the road – this car never sounded as if the motor was running – rich purple perfume drifted into the car. He was startled. He had thought somehow that flowers were fragrant only in the daytime. 'What do you want to do, Mace?' The front could probably seat four. Macey seemed ten feet away from him.

'I'm going to show Nana and Papa the photographs. I'm going to make them talk.'

He had never heard that tone of voice from her. Maybe from anybody. 'Mace?'

'How dare they!' Her voice was low and shuddering. 'How dare they bring me up to believe this is the best town in America, and we live on the best street, and our friends are the best people? How dare they tell me all fires blend together? That you could easily mix up that fire with any old beach bonfire? How dare they pretend they don't know what happened?'

Austin pulled into his grandparents' driveway. He did not share her rage. He felt terribly sad. His mother had said: it doesn't matter whether or not they started the fire; they're guilty. And now he believed this. Only the Beedons, whoever they were, had been good neighbours. The Fents and the Maceys and old Mr Collins and Vinnie Raspardo and the strangers in photo number seven had not been.

In a court of law, they could not be found guilty. But in a court of God?

The sugar maples and horse chestnut trees and red beech enclosed them in total dark.

How am I going to make it until Friday, when Dad comes? thought Austin. He pocketed the car keys and they walked back towards the Maceys'.

'I love Nana and Papa,' she whispered. 'Do you love your grandparents?'

'Everybody loves their grandparents.'

'I know, but . . . really.'

'Yes, really. They're stern, compared to yours, and they pay less attention, and they have other things to do, but they like having me, and they don't suggest that I should go back to my parents.'

'What is happening with your parents?'

He let out a long, controlled breath, as if making a candle flame shiver without blowing it out. 'My dad's coming this weekend. I don't know what he'll have to say. I don't know whether I'll stay here or go back to Chicago.'

'Stay,' said Macey.

'Oh, Mace!' he said, and he felt as if he were crumbling,

a cliff falling into the sea. 'I need my family. Maybe there's still a chance to keep us going. Venita lost all her chances. Whatever she could have been – and you and I were there when she was full of hope, hope for her church and the sixes and Shakespeare – she lost her chances. I don't know what Venita has given you, Mace. She gave me a calendar that could stop on any day of the week. Stop for ever.' He did not attempt a hug. He did not try to soften it. He said, 'I'm going home.'

The trumpets of a *Masterpiece Theatre* rerun were blaring, and Nana and Papa were happily involved with civilized Englishmen, magnificent country houses and splendid horses. 'Papa,' said Macey. 'Nana.'

'Macey,' said Nana, startled. 'And Austin. Have you two been out on a date?'

Macey actually smiled. It was so far from what a date ought to be. It might earn a slot in her own personal life record book: the worst evening spent with a great guy.

'Not exactly. Would you look at this photograph?'

She handed over the seventh shot. The fire illuminated the watchers as if there had been a multitude of flashbulbs. But you couldn't tell what they were doing. Without context, they could have posed for any reason.

Nana and Papa slid together on the sofa, adjusting their bifocals and moving the photograph back and forth to focus on it.

'My goodness,' said her grandfather, smiling, 'what memories that brings back! Where did you find this photo, Mace? This is many years ago. What's going on? What are we all doing there?'

Papa's smile tore at her heart. He was so sweet, such a teddy bear. But he was smiling at arson. 'I thought you could tell me,' said Macey. 'I know these are you two, and this is Austin's grandfather. Who are the others?'

'Well, that's Travis, somebody Travis, can't think of his first name. And that's, let me think, Philip Hammond, they must have left Shell Road forty years ago. Philip is dead, of course, but his wife remarried, she must be getting on in years. And this – think this is the little Yinson girl. Yes, and her husband. I haven't thought of the Yinsons in years. Now, what are they doing on our street? They lived across the creek, you know, on Brookside Drive.'

He dropped the photo and his face closed in. 'This is the night of that silly fire. Did you go on researching it?' His voice was full of reproach, as if Macey had been drowning puppies.

He is angry with *me*? 'It was started on purpose, Grandfather.' She had never called him anything but Papa. 'It was arson. It was meant to kill Wade Sibley.'

It's not Mr Sibley's story I'm researching, she thought. It isn't Venita's either. It is *mine*. I have to know what kind of people I come from. The good kind? Or the kind that pretend to be good? 'Tell me what happened that night.'

Her grandparents said nothing.

Big old drooly Moose pressed his nose against Macey. Aus collected the dog, rubbing ears and cheeks to keep Moose happy. Zipper slept on. Aus flicked off the television.

Macey stacked the dessert plates and coffee cups scattered on the coffee table. She dealt the photographs on to the coffee table, like Stella Miller in the nursing home, heavy and scary, demanding a card game and some truth.

'Macey, times were different then,' said her grandfather tiredly. 'We've all got to know better. Our attitudes have changed. We were prejudiced in those days, and it was wrong, and we have come a long way.'

Macey yanked herself upright, swirling around the coffee table, and Austin thought: She's learned it, her grandmother's flounce, that was perfect.

'Every time!' said Macey, twining her fingers to stop herself from hurling the dessert plates against the wall. 'Every single time I ask what happened, people change the subject. Even now you want to talk about how times have changed. I don't care how times have changed, Grandfather. I care about one night.'

She tapped the photograph of the melted mass that had been a car, until her grandparents were forced to look where her finger lay. 'Grandfather! *Did you start that fire?* Are you admiring your work?' she said fiercely.

He was aghast. He held up a trembling hand covered with age spots and a blue shiver of veins. He looked as old as Mr Collins. 'Macey! You can't think that.'

'I do think that.'

Her grandfather got to his feet, gripping the sofa edge for help. He was the same height as Macey and he glared into her face. 'I would never do such a thing. I am horrified that you are speaking to me like this. You ought to be ashamed of yourself!'

'Then how about my grandfather?' said Austin. 'Did he start it?'

'Nonsense.'

'Then who did?' said Macey.

'I don't think there was ever an investigation. The boy moved elsewhere, but it didn't drive him away, if that was the intent.'

'He wasn't a boy,' said Macey.

'Yes, he was. He was only twenty-two. Everybody thought he would be scared and run. Well, he was scared, but he didn't run. And I had to give him credit. In school, he never mentioned it to his students. Even to your mother, who was in his class. He never lashed out at the children. He conducted himself well.'

'I didn't ask that,' Macey said. 'I asked how *you* conducted *yourself*.'

To Austin, Macey looked like a goddess; a primitive creature of beauty and rage. If her short locks had turned to snakes, he would not have been surprised.

Austin thought: We're here at last. This is where we needed to come out. Not how Mr Sibley conducted himself. But how we conducted ourselves.

His need for his parents was so intense at that moment that he did not know how people grew up; how they went out into the world alone; how they survived at all.

'Where is Mr Sibley standing?' said Macey, tapping the lineup photo. 'You're wearing heavy jackets. It must have been very cold. Did you offer him a coat? Did you bring him a cup of coffee? Did he spend the night here?'

There was no answer.

'Your neighbour has no home, and no clothes, and no car, and no food, and no friends. Grandfather. What did you and Grandmother do?'

Her grandfather wilted. He took his wife's hand, the hand he had held for over half a century. He sank down beside her like a baked apple, getting smaller and lower and more wrinkled.

It was her grandmother who finally answered. 'We did nothing,' she said. 'We went back inside.'

They live in the right state, thought Austin. This is where we do nothing, and go back inside.

Austin's grandparents were not amused to be summoned into their own living room at almost midnight by two unsmiling teenagers.

'What have you two been up to? This is a ridiculous hour.'

'Either they wrecked the car or they're going to have a baby,' said his grandmother.

Austin actually felt his amazement at this remark. 'Once I learned that you were the banker who refused a checking account to Wade Sibley because he was black, Grandfather, I had to go on researching that barn fire.'

His grandfather's jaw lifted as if to duke it out with fists; as if his grandson planned to strike him and he planned to strike back. But Austin, who enjoyed fighting, who thought wrestling and boxing were great sports, was not up for combat tonight. He handed Macey's seven photographs to his grandfather. Grandfather looked at them without interest and passed them on to Austin's grandmother, who leafed through the same short stack.

'Times were different then,' said Grandfather irritably. 'There is no reason for you to stir the ashes. Those were ugly days, and we were witnesses to some of the ugliness. But it's ancient. It's history.'

'And were you just witnesses?'

'Exactly what do you mean by that?' snapped Grandfather.

'Did you start the fire?'

'You are completely out of line!' said his grandfather. 'We were asleep in bed, and when we got up, a fire was raging, and the occupant of the building was safely outside.'

'He wasn't an occupant,' said Macey. 'He was a man named Wade Sibley.'

Austin said, 'Why won't you just tell us what happened? What are you hiding, Grandfather?'

'I am hiding nothing!' His grandfather was deeply angry. Of course, it was not a prime moment, to have your only grandson accuse you of murder.

'That apartment should never have been rented to Wade Sibley,' said Grandmother. 'It was always rented to teachers, because teachers were good tenants. The landlords talked to the new science teacher over the phone, and he sounded like any other person; they had no idea he was going to turn out to be a coloured man. They were as shocked as anybody, and they apologized to us. They said they could just repaint after he moved out, buy new mattresses for the next tenant, and meanwhile we'd have to live with it.'

Austin had thought he was prepared for anything, but he was not prepared for that. 'Repaint? You mean he'd rub off on the apartment? They'd paint over where he touched?' Austin felt his dinner coming back up in his throat.

Macey stared at Mrs Fent and saw the two mommies who had been young in 1959: Monica and Leandra, with aprons and sturdy shoes and pincurls; saw them taking a casserole out of the oven, sliding spatulas under hot cookies. Heard them saying, 'But not for *that* neighbour, of course.'

How sexist I've been, thought Macey. I figured this was the responsibility of the men. But that's why my mother 'of course' never took cookies to Mr Sibley. Her mommy wouldn't let her.

Austin thought, It's the first of June. In one month and three days, my grandfather will turn eighty. We were going to have a joint birthday party: the USA's and Grandfather's, both July fourth. Fireworks and a brass quartet. Beach bonfires and all the relatives. How am I going to hug him on his eightieth birthday? How is he going to hug me?

Why did we do this? he thought, and he tried to remember, and all he could see was a small pink sneaker, square on the chest of laughing Isaiah.

'We had no involvement,' said Grandfather. 'We just stood there.'

'That's being involved,' said Macey. 'That's the worst kind of being involved.'

'Don't be melodramatic, Macey,' said Austin's grandmother.

'Did you help Mr Sibley, Mrs Fent?' she demanded. 'Did you offer him a place to stay?'

They offered me a place to stay, thought Austin. They are good people. But they are capable of bad things.

So this was history. A thing he and Macey could have left alone. Maybe should have left alone.

'You cannot possibly understand what it was like in those days,' his grandmother said. 'We didn't want a Negro in our house. None of it matters now.'

'All of it matters now,' said Austin. 'Who started the fire? You must have wondered. You must have made a guess.'

'Austin, nobody was hurt,' said his grandfather, 'and it was nothing but an old barn.'

And Wade Sibley, thought Austin, was nothing but a coloured man.

'There's no need to stir the ashes,' said Austin's grandmother. 'It won't change a minor event. Now it's late, and we all need to go to bed. If what you want is an apology for not wrapping our arms around the man in his hour of need, Macey, I give it to you. It was wrong of us.'

The moon had come out.

Sand and rock glittered. Clumps of wet beach grass shimmered. Water chattered over miles of beach and sandbar.

Austin walked Macey back to her grandparents' house.

He was betraying Macey, as her family's past had

betrayed her, but his decision to go home was so entire that he was afraid of her. She would be the only thing to keep him here, and he no longer wanted to be here.

They brushed against the lilac hedge. Thick purple scent choked the night air.

'When I met Venita,' said Macey slowly, looking at the sky and not at Austin, 'I felt a friendship coming through. Not the slow kind, where you know somebody all your life, and you sit near each other and the years pass. But the fast kind, where it's just there, and it's a privilege.'

She was no longer the goddess of revenge. She was someone thin and lonely. If he touched her, if he permitted himself one thought, one more breath of lilac, he would want to sit next to her and together let the years pass.

'I don't want you to go,' she said. 'But if you do . . .' Her voice wavered. 'Thank you for being a friend. Thank you for saving my life.'

And if he might have touched her, he would never know, because she did not look at him again, but held up her hand, a pale star of fingers in the dark, to stop him from speaking or following, and she walked on alone into her grandparents' house.

The porch gave her trouble.

The very same tall, round white pillar she touched for support had been in the seventh photograph, where neighbours admired a fire.

He was a friend of the privilege kind, she thought, and he'll be gone as completely as Venita. Just *gone*, and I can't stop them.

In the kitchen, her grandparents were waiting with smiles and a dessert.

Macey was scorched. Her love for Papa and Nana would never look or smell or feel the same.

And neither would the world.

She reached for the phone, dialling blindly, and when her mother answered sleepily, Macey realized how late it was; her parents, knowing she was at Nana and Papa's, had gone to bed. 'Mom, come and get me. Now.'

11

They came so quickly the tyres squealed on the pavement. 'What's the matter? What's going on?' said her father, half out of the car. 'What's going on?' said her mother, looking Macey up and down for damage.

Macey felt the way she had once described Austin: either ten years older or ten years younger. 'Wait till we're home, OK?'

Oh, Aus! she thought. My own history, one I can't save on a back porch, will start with a person who's leaving me.

She trudged into her house and, for the third time that night, dealt her pack of snapshots. What power the snapshots possessed! Mom gasped and stepped back from them.

Macey was too tired to stand any more, and she did not want hugs from these parents who had withheld so much truth, so she sat in a wooden chair with arms. 'You change the subject every time I ask, Mom. Now I have my grandparents' version. I have Austin's grandparents' version. What's yours?'

Her mother sank on to the rim of a matching chair, staring down at the pictures. 'It was a huge fire. Higher than the highest trees. It was so much more yellow and orange than you would expect, and so *ferocious*.

194

Howling and groaning. It was the noise that woke people. House by house, we poured out on to the street. It was shocking that a building with such great beams could be eaten as easily as a cupcake. Mr Sibley had got out safely. He was standing in pyjamas, barefoot, near the road. Nobody went near him. Nobody spoke to him. I didn't either. I didn't even think of it. He belonged there, in the dark at the side of the road. I didn't go inside to get him a coat or socks and shoes, and the next day in school I didn't go up to him and tell him how sorry I was.'

Dad came quickly to his wife's defence. 'You were a little kid,' he protested. 'You were thirteen.'

'Thirteen is old enough to help a neighbour.'

Thirteen was a terrible year; a year that travelled in packs, was brutally mean to anybody not part of the pack. And those neighbours lined up – what were they but a pack?

Jackals.

Would I have taken shoes to Mr Sibley? Macey wondered. Or stayed with the pack?

'And while the fire was raging,' said her mother, 'my parents were laughing with Austin's grandparents. They were best friends, remember. They did everything together. And my father said . . . "So, Henry, let's celebrate. Got any marshmallows?" And my mother went into the kitchen to get marshmallows, and when the fire died down a little, we all went over to toast a marshmallow to the removal of the Negro.'

Macey looked down at her lap. Well she had what she wanted. She knew the true colours of her family.

'I'm sorry you had to stumble on this, sweetheart,' said her father.

'I didn't stumble on it, Dad. I've been working for weeks to get here. And I'm not sorry.' This was a complete lie. Macey had never been so sorry about anything in her life. She felt like Stella Miller in the rest home, the world nothing but strangers and bad smells.

Austin was leaving.

Dad looked at her as if they had not met, or as if he had met somebody else named Macey. 'I knew you were investigating, and I let myself be amused. Isn't that sweet, my little girl with this little hobby of local history.'

'Nothing about this,' said Macey to her parents, 'has been sweet. That's even the word you used, Mom, when Mrs Framm said Bonnie became a science teacher in Mr Sibley's honour. It wasn't sweet, Mom, you shouldn't have said that.'

Her mother picked up photographs.

'It diminishes Mr Sibley,' agreed her father. 'That's what silence is for. To make somebody unimportant.'

So I can't be silent, thought Macey. But if I'm not silent, I have to be talking to somebody. About something. Like who? And what?

'That's one way to win in history,' her father said. 'You don't bother with battles and soldiers and gunpowder. You make a group of people unimportant, and they vanish, like an unpopular kid in the class.'

'Daddy, why haven't you said these things to me before? Were you ever going to? Were you going to let me grow up shallow and ignorant?'

196

'Shallow and ignorant are things we do well in this town,' said Mom.

'Then why are we here?' demanded Macey.

'I love this town,' said Mom. 'It's still the most beautiful place I've ever seen. However, its residents, and that includes us, don't always behave beautifully.'

'You're wrong,' said Macey. 'In this town, we do behave beautifully. That's why it works so well. Who would suspect, with such beauty and courtesy, that we are the kind of people who will take *any measure* to keep our town white?'

Her mother's patience ended. 'It happened once, Macey,' said Mom, sneaking a glance at her watch. '*Once*. Thirty-eight years ago. It's not a daily practice.'

'Daily practice,' said Macey, 'is how we make sure we don't have to use matches again.' If only Mom had not looked at her watch. *She loves us, see, but she can't quite be a mama*. Oh, Venita! thought Macey for the second time. Now I'm mad at you for saying things I'd remember!

'When you asked about segregation and the fifties, Mace,' said Dad, 'I just threw any old answers at you because the subject made me uncomfortable. I think maybe I let you down.'

'Yes. My whole family has let me down. My whole town. *My state.*'

Aus, she thought, hasn't let me down. But he's going in another direction, and it feels the same. I'm alone.

Mom patted herself in front of an invisible mirror, putting herself back together. 'What is it you really want, Macey?' she said.

That was easy. She wanted Aus. She wanted Venita

to have a real copy of Shakespeare. She wanted the crayons to be new.

She pressed the heels of her hands into her eyes to darken the star-bright image of Aus. She said, 'I want to know who started the fire. I will not be able to look at Nana and Papa unless I know who lit the match.'

'Oh, Macey!' said her mother, her tiny store of patience exhausted. 'I don't know! Nobody knows! Of course you can still look at Nana and Papa! I can't stand it when you get overly dramatic.'

Macey occupied herself with straightening the edges of her photographs.

Would she be as distant from Mom and Dad one day as Austin's mother was from *her* parents? Would Macey live in a faraway place, visit for a week in the summer, e-mail now and then, send a Christmas letter?

Her father clumsily tried to hug her, but he was standing and she was sitting and it didn't work. She did not do the things required to improve the hug – stand, turn, reach, cuddle.

On top of everything else, thought Macey, I have to find another research project and get it done by the end of the week.

Austin's father did not wait till Friday. He flew in the following morning. And Austin went home with his father.

Macey and Aus had to say goodbye in front of four deeply angry grandparents; in front of her own mother and father, who were treating her like a stranger; and in front of Austin's father, who was a stranger.

It stung that Aus had not managed this better.

But his face was lit up, his step bouncing. She had never seen Aus so happy, his head tilting back because the laughter was so complete. He loves his father, she thought.

She wanted Austin to have that: a love whole and solid, the kind where they came on the plane to get you.

Macey pulled her neighbour close and touched her lips to his cheek. 'I'm happy you're happy, Aus.'

The thing was not to cry.

'We're coming back in July,' said his dad cheerfully. 'Like always. I'm going to stay this time. We'll be here for two weeks. Austin's grandfather is going to give us both sailing lessons. Pray for good weather and lots of wind.'

July was not a windy month. And how could it be like always? Would Austin's mother come too? What family was he going back to? Did he know? Did either of them know?

But who knows a family? thought Macey. I didn't know mine.

She touched Austin's shoulder and whispered, 'Safe flight,' and he said, 'I'll see you in July,' and they were gone.

When Dad said, 'Would you come back with me?' Austin didn't pause a moment. There was no thinking to be done, no considerations, no weighing one side or another. 'Yes,' he said.

'I've been a crummy father,' said Dad. 'That's all there is to it. My life caved in, and I was glad to see my kid go, because then I could concentrate on how crummy my life was. And when we talked, and you needed me, it turned out I had to be on the next plane.'

That his father had not waited; that Dad dropped everything, grabbed a taxi, rushed to O'Hare Airport, found a plane, any plane, to take him to his son – it erased all the months of separation. 'Is Mom living at the house still?' said Austin anxiously. 'Will she be there when we get home?'

'She's picking us up at the airport.'

Aus was so glad. 'You two are back together?'

'I didn't say that. I said she was picking us up at the airport.'

'Oh. What does that mean?'

'It means she'll have a car, Aus. But we've both missed you terribly, and we're both sorry we let you go so easily and missed a whole school year of you.' When his father gave a hug, it was quick and fierce, but now the hugs came in a row, one after another, as if Dad were counting out the days they'd missed.

'You sure it's OK to leave before the end of the school year?' asked Dad.

'It's OK.' Aus hugged his father back, and when he thought of Mom waiting for them at the airport, he didn't care about anything that had gone wrong; not one harsh word mattered. He just wanted to see her.

'And Macey?' said his father tentatively.

Aus didn't want to talk about Macey. So he just nodded.

It stabbed him that he was leaving her. She needed an ally, and he was the only one, and if she decided to wage a war now, she would fight alone.

He would have fought alongside her if he had stayed. But Austin was not making war. He was making peace.

As for Grandfather, Austin still ached to be the kid Grandfather could do neat things with. But that was gone.

The plane took off.

It would land in his city; his state.

Austin loved take-off. Planes leaving the ground never seemed to be going fast enough, and the sense of risk, which he loved, enveloped him, and his pulse rose, and he wished he could be the pilot.

He had a sense of leaving a legacy to Macey: Mr Sibley in 1959 and Venita in 1997 were hers now.

The plane reached thirty thousand feet, and the clouds below them were solid, and the world Macey occupied was as unreachable as the past.

The sky was like candy, pink with disappearing sun. The sun slid lower in the sky and pink became blood-red. The bright green leaves of the trees grew dark against the sky, losing their colour, just cool shadow.

Graff said, 'Mace? I'm closing.'

She struggled to focus on him. She had not known she was in the media centre. She had not known there were people around her. She'd been staring out the window, falling into the alone of her life.

'What were you looking up?' asked Graff. 'I hated to disturb you.'

She got up unsteadily, as awkward as that seventh-grader whose arms stuck out too far, and whose legs banged together when she walked. 'Just fooling around

201

with that site that has every phone number in the USA.'

'Yeah? Who'd you find? Somebody cool?'

She shook her head. 'I don't know yet. Thank you for staying open for me.' She put one foot in front of the next. Then she picked up another foot and stuck it ahead, too. It was a plan. Eventually she would reach a phone.

There was a phone in the massive front lobby. Actually, there were six phones. The school building wouldn't close just because the media centre was closing; there were athletic events and night classes and meetings. She could telephone people indefinitely. She leaned against the wall and thought: I can do this. I can even do it alone. I don't have to have Aus with me. Although I wouldn't mind. Although I'd love it.

She picked up a phone. She tapped in her credit card number. She tapped in the California number she'd got off the Internet.

A man answered.

'May I please speak to Mr Wade Sibley?'

'This is Wade Sibley.'

'You're not angry, Mr Sibley?' she said. 'I'm angry.'

'Of course you're angry. I was angry for years. But it wore off. Go easy on your mother, Macey. She was thirteen. It's not a brave age. You don't have the courage, when you're thirteen, to stand up to your parents and your whole neighbourhood.'

Her grandparents had not been thirteen. They could have stood up if they'd wanted. There had been only one couple with courage. 'Who were the Beedons, anyway? I didn't find them.'

'The Beedons,' said Mr Sibley, 'were deacons in the church. I met them the one Sunday I attended. They'd had me over for dinner. They got an anonymous phone call about the fire, and they drove down and asked if they could take me in while things were sorted out. That's the phrase people used. While things were sorted out. What it meant was, while we figure out who wanted to burn you up and whether they'll try again.'

Macey did not want to ask why he had gone to church only once. She did not want one more hard answer. 'Austin wanted to know about your bare feet.'

'The junior-high faculty came through for me. The shoes were from a gym teacher, who brought two pairs. The music teachers scraped together all they could spare – in those days, teachers were paid very little and took me shopping for clothing. The principal gave me a car that had been meant for his daughter, but the daughter said she didn't need one as much as I did.'

She was swept by relief. 'So *some* people helped.'

'Some people helped,' agreed Wade Sibley, 'and I have a soft spot in my heart for them. But it wasn't enough. All winter, I'd say to myself, Why am I teaching these kids? Why am I investing my life *here*? And there was no answer. I left, to teach elsewhere. I believe that the fire of December 1959 left a burn mark on me and on the town that has never been erased.'

'There is so much in this story!' Macey said. 'Why didn't you go public? You could have been a guest on every talk show in the world!'

'The talk show wasn't invented yet. And the fire *was* public, Macey, and I could gauge reaction by looking at the neighbours. It was not a topic people wanted. That was the point of the fire. They wanted me and it – meaning race – to go away.'

She quit trying not to cry, and if some tears were over Austin and some were for herself, maybe that was OK. Mopping her face on her sleeve, she said, 'The thing I really need you to tell me is, who started the fire?'

There was a long pause. Then Mr Sibley said gently, 'Macey, I have only guesses. No facts. We're not going to know now, unless somebody confesses, and it's clear from your research that nobody is going to. I think it would be best for you to forget about who did it.'

How terrible to be speaking with the only other person on earth who cared who started the fire – and to know what he was doing. Saving Macey from the truth.

It is my grandfather, thought Macey. Mr Sibley wouldn't bother otherwise.

'Mr Sibley,' she said, 'may I tell you about another fire? Do you have time to hear about a girl named Venita, who died?'

'Yes.'

She liked how Mr Sibley answered. He didn't step away. He said yes. Austin answered like that. One syllable. *Austin was gone*.

She told him about Venita and a friendship that had been the privilege kind. She told him about Saturday Group, the stubs of crayons, the children without toilet seats at school, and the photocopies of *Hamlet*. She told him about the fire and the shooting and the letter from Dorothy Edna Loomis.

She began to feel strangely cheerful. At last she had an audience who would care, who would look up for a moment, pay attention. 'I feel as if I have a promise to keep, Mr Sibley,' she finished. 'But what?'

'Why don't you call Reverend Warren and ask him?' said Mr Sibley briskly. 'He's right there, he can tell you what your high school can do, what your friends can do, where the money is needed, where the attention should be brought, what the television station should be filming, where to take the governor, what to tell to the legislature.'

She almost let go of the telephone, as if it were carrying a virus. As if the voice coming out of it was going to trap her. 'You're kidding,' she said, trying to laugh. This was not what he was supposed to say.

'Macey, you found out everything you need to know. Life isn't fair. Silence doesn't help. Good neighbours have to step in. If nobody drives down the road to help the guy who lost his house, he can't go on. And if nobody goes back to Venita's world and makes sure crayons are whole and the pavements are safe, none of those little kids can go on either.'

She had expected him to tell her how good she was. How her heart, as opposed to older, crueler hearts, was in the right place. She felt attacked. She tried to brush his words away. 'Mr Sibley, I can't solve the problems of the world.'

'Nobody has figured out how to solve the problems of the world. But you got your assignment from Mrs Loomis. You have to try. Otherwise there's no privilege left in the friendship with Venita. Not unless you step forward.'

Step forward. Step forward where? There were no steps for Macey Clare to take. She tried to end the conversation courteously. 'And – are you still teaching, Mr Sibley? Do you – um – still like teaching?'

'Oh, I see,' said Mr Sibley. 'You were hoping to settle the past with this phone call. Because the past is *their* responsibility. You aren't too happy to have me bring up the present. Because the present – that's *your* responsibility. And you'd rather step aside.'

Macey wanted to throw things at him. Unfortunately, telephones did not yet have the capacity for that. 'I wasn't involved,' she said. 'I didn't do anything.'

'Isn't that your grandparents' line?'

She wanted nothing except to get off the phone. Pretend she had never made this call. Never heard these words. What had happened to that understanding teacher who told her not to be hard on her mother? 'I'm alone,' she said pleadingly, trying to make him understand what it was to be alone.

'You won't be alone once you start.'

'That's easy for you to say. You don't know this town.'

'Actually, I know that town pretty well.'

She had forgotten. Nobody knew as thoroughly as Wade Sibley what it was to be alone.

'Your town has enough good guys,' he said. 'You're going to be the first in line, and it's a scary position, but you can hold it down. Recruit some allies. How about Lindsay and Grace?'

'Are you kidding? They'd just laugh.'

'About what?'

'That any of it matters. That Venita mattered. That she was even a person.'

'Then you should start with them,' said Mr Sibley.

The man knew nothing. He was decades ago. He did not understand a thing. She would lose her friends. People would not meet her eyes. They would not sit with her. She would be a jerk. She would be alone.

Play with fire, she thought, and get your fingers burned. Who reached into the ashes? I did. It isn't a grandparent who will get burned. My grandparents and Austin's – they'll just stand back from the fire and wait, like they did before. I will get burned.

But Mr Sibley was saying goodbye, and what he said was, 'Godspeed.'

After the night of the photographs, Mom and Dad changed their work hours and got home on the 5:40 instead of the 7:08, so Macey had dinner with her parents on weeknights, which was rare. This lasted two evenings. Then it was back to routines.

Nana phoned. 'Darling, Papa will come get you, we're having rosemary garlic chicken.'

'No, thanks, I'm fine here,' said Macey.

But Papa came anyway, so she was courteous and let Papa hug her, but she was not a little girl with a perfect grandfather. She was a sad young woman hugged by a sad old man.

She found if she sat rather still and kept a stiff posture, like a woman in a nineteenth-century daguerreotype, that Mr Sibley's words could be kept at a distance. She was reconstructing the phone call in her mind, taking hold of the nice friendly parts at the beginning and abandoning the hard parts at the close.

Grace had got her driver's licence and a seven-year-old Blazer.

Lindsay's aunt Joyce was going to take Lindsay to France for a month during the summer, so there was a ton of shopping to do, and they went in Grace's Blazer, and helped Grace with traffic and parallel parking.

'So . . . how were things between you when Austin left?' said Grace.

Macey shrugged.

'You can't get away with that,' said Lindsay. 'We'll ask you yes-and-no questions so you don't have to talk much and you won't start crying, but you have to answer. First question. Did you know he was going?'

Nod.

'Did he tell you and was he nice about it?'

Nod.

'Is he coming back?'

Macey wanted to believe that she and Aus would have some lovely long-distance relationship, with e-mail and cards and phone calls and visits, and she would fly to Chicago to go to his prom, and eventually they'd attend the same college . . . but she doubted it. The year had got too hard for Austin. Everything came down upon his shoulders like a building being demolished, and Austin had stepped out of the rubble and left. If he came back, he wouldn't be the same Austin.

Macey began sobbing and her two friends tried to hug, tried to comfort, but the Blazer, like life, had too many obstructions; things were in the way; the hugs couldn't quite hold.

School drew to a close. Everybody was on a countdown. Ten days of school left.

Nine.

Eight.

In the media centre, Macey attempted railroad research. She had no more interest in it than Aus had had.

The place was crammed with other kids in the same situation. Since Macey was the kind of kid who started assignments the day they were given and neatly spread the work over the weeks allotted, she had never hung out with the kids who pretended there was no assignment until the day before it was due.

That, however, turned out to be much more fun than doing it the regular way.

The media centre was one big party.

Graff had bought soda – the cheap Brand X kind that nobody liked, except in desperate circumstances like this – and boxes of Nilla Wafers, pointless cardboard cookies that nobody liked either, but if you had one, you'd attack the whole box, and even hide the rest from other people so they couldn't have any of yours.

Austin had got most of his stuff from history books and volumes on transportation. Going online was so much more fun than using books on the shelf. Macey and a dozen other kids had to wait for a free terminal.

'Rachel,' said Jennifer, 'are you giving the speech on Sophomore Class Day?'

Rachel was academically first in the class. 'I'm

planning to come down with glandular fever,' said Rachel. 'I just have to finish this project and get it in on time, and then I'll quickly get a fever and some fatigue and need to be home for several days, especially the one my speech is scheduled on.'

Everybody laughed. Half the time the speakers for Class Day got sick. People pretended to be sympathetic, but the sickness was better known as panic. Who on earth would want to stand up in front of four hundred classmates and talk about truth and the future for fifteen minutes? Or fifteen seconds, for that matter?

'I wanted to be first in the class,' said Jennifer, 'and my parents ordered me to be first, but my rank is eleven, and the good news is, no matter how many people get sick, I am not going to have to give a speech.'

'It's sort of like the royal family,' said Matt, who was fourth in the class. 'An awful lot of them would have to die in a plane crash for you to be the one who gets the throne.'

'You might,' said Rachel thoughtfully.

'No, because I have a low blood count too,' said Matt. 'The thought of getting up on that stage and facing the toughest audience on earth on the toughest subject on earth – the meaning of life and school – is enough to give anybody a low blood count.'

The meaning of life and school, thought Macey. She was slumped over and jammed up, and her defence of perfect posture failed her: Every word that Wade Sibley had spoken began grinding through her mind, like a long train on a long track.

'Move, Macey,' said Jennifer, 'you're next in line. Take Shannon's seat.' Jennifer pushed Macey in front of the same computer she'd crashed the day she shut it down too fast after reading about Adam Devers.

Macey slung her bag by its straps over the chair and noodled around to a search engine. If she typed 'railroads', there'd be a million hits. She had to think of parameters.

Adam Devers, she thought.

'I'm supposed to talk for fifteen minutes,' said Rachel. 'Do you have any idea how long fifteen minutes is? I slaved over a speech, and when I timed it, it's two minutes and twenty seconds long.'

Adam Devers. Macey's spine crawled. Her hands iced. Her head seemed too heavy to hold up.

'That's as long as we want to listen,' Jennifer assured her.

Everybody laughed and made disgusting suggestions for what to do with the other twelve minutes and forty seconds.

Macey found the newspaper site. She scrolled to the obituary index. Once more she read the brief notice of the suicide of Adam Devers.

November 30, 1960.

Almost one year to the day after the fire.

Alice and Adam Devers had expected to get the barn apartment, but instead they'd been stuck living in that teensy house with her parents. And Adam had to teach with the coloured man who got their apartment. Had to share a desk and a lab with this man – a teacher so popular that his students could remember his lesson

211

plans thirty-eight years later – a man whose presence was so revolting that the landlord intended to repaint after he left.

Alice had said, No, we didn't go over – we don't gawk at fires. But they were in that photograph, staring at the fire along with the rest of the neighbours.

Could Adam Devers have been the arsonist?

Macey had found it hard to credit that white people in Arkansas and Mississippi and Georgia and North Carolina had been so brutal. She could hardly imagine the stoning of black children, the closing of schools, the rioting, the lynching. She could believe it only in a history-book kind of way.

She had not believed that it could happen here (where, everybody pointed out, we were always civilized). Even after all her research and pondering, she had not believed. And here it was.

Oh, Adam Devers! she thought. You did a terrible thing, and you knew it, and you had no way to undo it. So you had to undo yourself. You celebrated the anniversary of your fire. You buried yourself.

Macey took a handful of Nilla Wafers for sustenance and made it to the hall. Then she took up a floor position on the carpet, for no reason except her legs felt too weak to carry her home.

It was not Nana and Papa who had lit the match.

It was not Austin's grandmother and grandfather.

She ought to feel pretty good, knowing that she did not have an arsonist in the family; that whatever else their true colours were, they weren't the colours of people who tried to kill by fire.

But even though she had probably found out the truth, she did not know anybody who cared.

Nana and Papa, Mr and Mrs Fent, Mom and Dad – all six of them didn't care.

He wasn't our kind, so who cares? Stop being dramatic about this, Macey – the guy is black. We didn't care what happened to him in 1959, we didn't care once in all the years that came to pass, and we sure don't care now in 1997.

I care, thought Macey. If Venita hadn't died, would I care? If Mrs Loomis hadn't sent a letter, would I care?

And what good does it do to care? Caring doesn't change anything.

She braced her hands on the carpet to keep herself rigid and controlled. She felt like carpet herself: low, muddy and stuck to the floor. The last time she'd sat here, it had been with Austin.

Oh, Aus! she thought. I can call you about this, and you'll be polite, and you'll say the right things, but when I call you, I want it to be about us. Not this.

When I call. Was she that sure? Would she really call him?

She thought about bravery. *The toughest audience on earth on the toughest subject on earth*. And twelve minutes and forty seconds had just become available.

Macey could take on that audience. She could say: We can do better than stir ashes. Our true colours don't have to be not-thinking colours. Silent colours. We do not have to stand on the side of the road in the dark, like our parents and grandparents. If we don't drive down the road to help the guy who lost his house, he

213

can't go on. And if we don't go back to Venita's world and make sure the crayons are whole, and the pavements are safe, none of those little kids can go on either.

But Macey Clare didn't have the guts to sell grapefruit for the band. She was going to get up in front of that crowd? Oh, please. The Lisas of the world would avoid her, and every Max and Jennifer, every kid she knew, even Lindsay and Grace, would find other friends.

She mocked herself with newspaper headlines: White Girl Tries to Save World.

What would Venita do if she were here? Giggle?

Or say, What took you so long?

Or say, Girl, you think you can accomplish anything?

She thought of the power of photographs, of slides.

Isaiah would take slides for her. Here's their bathroom. Here's our bathroom. Here's their backyard. Here's ours. Here's their media centre. Here's ours. Would that be the way to handle it? With pictures? Pictures of a burning barn had certainly spoken to Austin and Macey.

Oh, Aus! she thought. How could you make me do this alone? How could you have left me here by myself?

'Mace?' said Lindsay anxiously. 'Are you OK? What's the matter?'

Lindsay was kneeling beside her. Grace was handing over a tissue. Macey had not known she was crying.

I'm not giving any speeches, thought Macey. I can't believe I thought of it for a second. It would be insane. As long as you shut up, you get to stay friends with everybody and laugh at the in-jokes. Ashes don't burn, friends don't get on planes. You keep your secrets, the years pass, secrets get smaller, and you don't care any more. It didn't matter anyway, you say to yourself.

'End-of-the-year syndrome,' said Lindsay sympathetically. 'Have a shopping spree, I say. That solves anything.'

If only Macey had some idea how to solve anything at all.

So you be true, and you run for Venita. Use that life you have.

Macey sighed. She hadn't felt the hands of the Lord. It would be easier if she had. 'I'm going to go to the principal,' she said to Grace, 'and ask if I can share Rachel's speech time. I certainly have twelve minutes and forty seconds' worth of stuff to say.'

Grace looked steadily back. 'On what topic, Mace?'

'Burning. I finally understand, Grace. It took me so long! I'm so slow! It isn't the barn burning in 1959 that matters. It's that *we're still on fire.* When I stirred the ashes, it didn't start a fire. Fire has been burning all along. We're going to burn down our own house if we don't put out the fire.'

Grace took a deep breath, lowered her eyelids and opened them wide again.

'What are you talking about, Macey?' said Lindsay.

But Grace said, 'Think first, Mace. Nobody wants this. You start this up, they won't want you either.'

Macey felt closer to Grace than she ever had, because what was a friend for, if not to give warning? Everybody in this school, this town and this state,

215

wanted to stand by the side of the road in the dark. She said, 'Grace, I don't see how I can do it alone. Come with me.'

They stared at each other.

Lindsay was confused and hurt. 'Macey. What are you talking about?'

'The fire of hate,' said Macey. 'Somehow . . . it turned out to be my job. Putting it out.'

Grace shook her head. 'Forget it, Mace. You can't put out racial fires.'

'But if I don't try, or take a first step, I can't ever call Mr Sibley back, or think about Venita, or reread Dorothy Edna Loomis's letter, or send another box of crayons to Good Shepherd.'

'Oh, that,' said Lindsay. She stood up, dusting her hands on her jeans.

Macey's heart hurt. What if everyone in school – like her grandparents, like her parents, like Lindsay – said, 'Oh, that,' and dusted themselves off and walked away?

But Lindsay put out both hands, one to each friend, and hauled Macey and Grace to their feet.

'Oh, *brother*,' said Grace irritably. 'OK, fine, we're friends, we'll go with you to the principal. He'll probably agree. You'll get your twelve minutes and forty seconds. Just don't say I didn't warn you. Nobody cares, Mace.'

'Going to the office is not the hard part. I need you to stand on the stage with me when I give my talk.'

'Oh, *brother!*' moaned Grace. 'I'm not standing anywhere with you if you're going to preach. I can feel a disaster coming. I won't be part of it.'

But that's the point, isn't it? thought Macey. Brotherhood. If we don't talk about it, we won't have it.

'Disaster has been here all along,' she said softly. 'We *are* part of it, Grace.'

And Mr Sibley had known after all where to start finding allies, because Grace nodded, and so did Lindsay, and the three of them went down the hall together.

There were fires to put out.